THE LAW
OF THE WHITE
CIRCLE

THE LAW
OF THE WHITE
CIRCLE

A Novel by
THORNWELL JACOBS

Foreword by
W. FITZHUGH BRUNDAGE

Supplementary Readings by
PAUL STEPHEN HUDSON,
WALTER WHITE, and W. E. B. DU BOIS

The University of Georgia Press
Athens & London

Paul Stephen Hudson's "'Immovable Folkways': Thornwell Jacobs's
The Law of the White Circle and the Atlanta Race Riot of 1906" originally
appeared in *Georgia Historical Quarterly* 83 (Summer 1999): 293–313
and appears here courtesy of the Georgia Historical Society. The excerpt
from *A Man Called White: The Autobiography of Walter White* is from pages
5–12 of the University of Georgia Press edition (Athens, 1995) and
appears courtesy of Jane White Viazzi.

Library of Congress Cataloging-in-Publication Data

Jacobs, Thornwell, 1877–1956.
The law of the white circle : a novel / by Thornwell Jacobs ;
foreword by W. Fitzhugh Brundage ; supplementary readings by
Paul Stephen Hudson, Walter White, and W. E. B. Du Bois.
p.   cm.
ISBN-13: 978-0-8203-2880-5 (pbk. : alk. paper)
ISBN-10: 0-8203-2880-4 (pbk. : alk. paper)
1. Race riots—Georgia—Atlanta—History—20th century—
Fiction. 2. Atlanta (Ga.)—Race relations—Fiction. 3. African
Americans—Fiction. I. Title.
PS3519.A42L39 2006
813'.52—dc22   2006010727

British Library Cataloging-in-Publication Data available

www.ugapress.org

CONTENTS

FOREWORD

W. Fitzhugh Brundage

Nothing that had happened in Atlanta since its capture by Sherman's army during the Civil War had greater national significance than the riot in the fall of 1906. By no means was the Atlanta riot the first mass attack against blacks in a southern city. Race riots had erupted with tragic regularity in such places as Norfolk, New Orleans, Memphis, and Vicksburg during Reconstruction. But with Reconstruction's end and the return of "white rule" during the 1880s, more than a decade passed before the mounting toll of lynching and the 1898 antiblack pogrom in Wilmington, North Carolina, highlighted a dramatic deterioration in American race relations. Yet, even at a time when both virulent racist rhetoric and racial violence were becoming commonplace, the Atlanta race riot was an unprecedented cataclysm.

Atlanta, after all, was the exemplary city of the New South. Boasting pluck that even Yankees admired, Atlantans after the Civil War rebuilt their city into one of the nation's major railroad hubs and distribution centers. Atlanta's entrepreneurial spirit had been translated into a creed of regional uplift and national reconciliation by Henry Grady, Atlanta's most distinguished newspaperman. And it was at the Cotton States Exposition in Atlanta in 1895 that Booker T. Washington had delivered his most celebrated address. In his so-called "Atlanta Compromise" speech, Washington summarized his program of education, self-help, and racial cooperation. To the delight of his white listeners, he seemingly renounced social integration of the races and advocated that blacks and whites work separately for their common good. When Washington delivered his Atlanta speech, he believed that he was striking a bargain with whites, not surrendering to them. In return for white aid for greater educational and economic opportunity, Washington proposed an interracial "compromise" that would resolve the status of blacks in the South. To observers, Atlanta at the dawn of the twentieth century, with its robust and forward-looking entrepreneurial spirit, burgeoning black business district, and cluster of noted black colleges, was the model southern city where black and white southerners lived according to both Grady's and Washington's teachings.

When white rioters launched their attacks along Decatur Street on September 22, 1906, they shattered most assumptions about Atlanta's inevitable progress and its enviable racial harmony. Not until after five days of rioting, killing, and property destruction did white authorities restore order. Previously, white southerners had reassured themselves that the savagery of lynch mobs was the lamentable but justifiable (and inevitable) response of white men to the criminality of black men. The indiscriminate nature of the Atlanta riot, however, belied such claims: all blacks, regardless of class, sex, character, or demeanor, were targets of the marauding mobs. In this instance, Americans glimpsed the terrifying reality of the "race war" that pessimistic observers periodically predicted for the nation's future.

During and especially after the riot, Americans struggled to make sense of it. One of these Americans was W. E. B. Du Bois. On the riot's first day, as he made his way from Alabama back to the city, Du Bois composed his heartrending lament "A Litany of Atlanta." Local blacks in general, however, had to display extreme caution when making public their perspective on and outrage about the riot. When J. Max Barber, editor of the *Voice of the Negro*, sent an anonymous telegram to the *New York World* describing the carnage, some of Atlanta's leading white citizens warned Barber to leave the city immediately. Years later, Walter White, a leader of the National Association for the Advancement of Colored People, vividly recalled in his autobiography the composure and resolve that his father and other blacks showed in the face of white mobs. For White, the riot was a telling illustration of the life-and-death importance of black communal organization. In the wake of the riot, Booker T. Washington also looked for a silver lining in the tragedy. He hastened to the city, anxious to somehow turn the trouble into a pretext for interracial cooperation. But Washington's appeals to the "better sorts" of both races to forge an alliance against crime and violence offered no justice to the riot's victims and fueled growing disenchantment among blacks skeptical of Washington's program. In contrast, many white Atlantans found in the riot confirmation of the need for a crackdown on alleged black criminality and for sterner enforcement of racial segregation. Outside observers also were acutely interested in the riot. By early November, Ray Stannard Baker, one of the nation's preeminent muckraking reporters, had begun the first systematic investigation of the riot's origins. His influential account,

which traced the riot to tensions that flared when criminally prone rural blacks and displaced rural whites faced
off in the South's new cities, appeared first in *American
Magazine* in 1907 and a year later in a compilation of his
articles titled *Following the Color Line.*

This same urge to explain the events prompted
Thornwell Jacobs to travel to Atlanta within days of the
riot and to write *The Law of the White Circle.* Published
in the same year as Baker's much better-known work,
Jacobs's novella encapsulated the political, social, and racial worldview of the "best" southern whites in whom both
Henry Grady and Booker T. Washington had placed so
many of their hopes. The son of a noted cleric, Jacobs had
completed seminary at Princeton and briefly presided
over a Presbyterian Church in North Carolina before pur-
suing a publishing career in Nashville. By no means was
Jacobs a reactionary thinker. Rather he was an exemplar
of the New South who was comfortable with progress, education, economic modernization, and current wisdom
in the social and natural sciences.

His story's plot is straightforward. Recounting the strat-
agems of Lola, a light-skinned elite mulatta, to "pass" as a
white woman, Jacobs highlights the urban anonymity of
Atlanta that makes possible a racial mixing that contra-
dicts primordial laws of racial separateness. Eventually, as
though motivated by a group instinct that defies articula-
tion, whites resort to "jungle justice" to restore the proper
distance between the races. The novella concludes when
Lola's true racial identity is revealed and her white suitor
renounces her with the parting words of "Go back to your
people." *The Law of the White Circle* exploits many tropes
of turn-of-the-century melodrama, including improbable

but dramatic plot twists and the stock character of the tragic mulatto, whose ambiguous racial identity is the source of inappropriate and ultimately dangerous longings. Neither on grounds of literary innovation nor artistry does *The Law of the White Circle* warrant much attention. The plight of mulattoes "passing" was commonplace in an age when bloodlines were presumed to dictate personal destiny. And thwarted love had long been a melodrama staple. Even Jacobs conceded the stilted character of his work when he informed the reader at the novella's outset that his book was offered as "a sociological study, not a 'problem novel.'"

In producing such a study, Jacobs succeeded, though largely in revealing and profoundly disturbing ways that he did not anticipate. Although his intent was to explain the impulses that drove whites to resort to "jungle justice," he actually ended up compiling the lines of thought that elite white southerners embraced to justify white supremacy. Jacobs, as Paul Stephen Hudson explains, translated contemporary sociological and anthropological theories about innate racial differences and the evolutionary hierarchy of races into a melodrama of apocalyptic race war. The lesson to be drawn from *The Law of the White Circle* would seem to be clear: racial separation is the only possibility for the coexistence of two inherently antagonistic races. The best outcome that can be imagined for the "race problem" is a nervous truce, maintained by the "better elements" of both races. Apparently, Jacobs could not see far enough in the future to imagine a time when those of the "white circle" might acknowledge the common humanity of all races. Nor did the "law of the white circle" provide any prospect that calls for racial equity or social justice would be answered, because such appeals evidently would fly in the face of inexorable natural laws. Here then is as pessimistic a prognosis for the nation and its people as we are likely to encounter in American fiction.

The lasting significance of Jacobs's novella was not its critical and popular success—it enjoyed a measure of both—but its stark and concise encapsulation of a white worldview that today is, thankfully, seldom heard in public. By reading *The Law of the White Circle*, we can understand better the mind-set of the architects of Jim Crow as well as its defenders during the 1950s and 1960s. A half century after the publication of Jacobs's book, white southern leaders, many of whom boasted of their progressive leanings, invoked a version of the "law of the white circle" when they defended segregation as the only means to secure racial peace. If segregation was abolished, they argued, lower-class whites would take matters into their own hands, and the South would be gripped by race war. And when white parents expressed horror at the prospect of their children fraternizing with black peers in public schools and when white ministers appealed to the laws of nature to condemn "racial mixing" in nightclubs and public spaces, they were all drawing on the deep reservoir of racist ideology that Thornwell Jacobs and his ilk had fashioned at the dawn of the twentieth century.

Five years before Jacobs published *The Law of the White Circle*, W. E. B. Du Bois, then a resident and college professor in Atlanta, published his acclaimed *The Souls of Black Folk*. With remarkable prescience, Du Bois predicted that "the problem of the Twentieth Century is the problem of the color-line." Although Jacobs was separated by the chasm of racial identity and life experience from Du Bois, he undoubtedly agreed that nothing was so likely to vex the American nation as the problem of race. Reading *The Law of the White Circle* at the dawn of the twenty-first century offers sobering insight into the values of a society that could unleash the dark forces of a rioting mob and then justify them as inevitable. Yet reading Jacobs's novella also fosters a degree of hope that the virtual abolition of "the law of the white circle" has demonstrated that America's racial problem is not immutable.

Gathered together in this edition are some of the most troubling and revealing cultural artifacts of the Atlanta riot. As though in dialogue, Thornwell Jacobs's white supremacist novella is juxtaposed with W. E. B. Du Bois's pleading contemporaneous lament, Walter White's measured but vivid recollections of the riot from his childhood perspective, and Paul Hudson's astute scholarly survey of the historical and intellectual context that inspired Jacobs to set pen to paper in the riot's wake. Of course, not even these gathered documents can fully explain the paroxysm of rage and violence that gripped Atlanta in 1906. But there is almost certainly no better place to start than with this edition of *The Law of the White Circle*.

THE LAW
OF THE WHITE
CIRCLE

"She would be burned at the stake if they discover her!" he muttered.

THE LAW
OF THE WHITE
CIRCLE

By

THORNWELL JACOBS

Author of
"Sinful Sadday,"
"The Shadow of Attacoa"

With Illustrations by

GILBERT GAUL, N.A.

DEDICATION

To my dear old father, who could have written it so much better than I have done, who will see some good in it, although the whole world scoffs, this story is dedicated.

TO THE READER

There are probably very few people of good sense who would care to write a story of race conflict and riot. For myself it has not been a pleasure, but a duty. It has seemed to many of us that those novelists who have chosen the subject have spent too large a part of their time in expostulations concerning negro inferiority, and too little in arraignment of our white lepers who have converted a disaster into dynamite. The object of this book is not to call the negro a "black brute" and the Aryan a "white angel," but to give a fair interpretation of those tremendous agencies which are making our national race problem a pall or a powder mine, as Providence may determine. *The Law of the White Circle* is a sociological study, not a "problem novel;" and if read in a spirit of thoughtful fairness, perhaps an excuse may be found for its existence. It is not intended to please nor to dazzle, but to make its readers think—perhaps to help them understand "The End."

Nashville, Tenn., October 1, 1908.

CONTENTS

7

CHAPTER I

Son of the South Mountains

The Wa-haws were called the "South Mountains" before the days of Roy Keough. Roy changed many things about Dunvegan—among others, a tradition or two—and had a way of giving a purplish hue to things. After he had come and gone, men described him as a "see-er," and stated that his whole reputation came from his ability to look past the phenomena into the soul of persons and events; but while he was in Dunvegan he was only a "son of the South Mountains."

"Kee-o" his father had always thought was the way to spell the family name until Colonel Russell, who had bought the Dunvegan *Democrat* from the Preston heirs, mentioned "the big red apples that grew in the South Mountains. It is a shame that such a country should be the home of heathen. They say that the Keoughs and Crawfords have not been to church for five years."

Roy Keough, Sr., to whom this was read, took all print as complimentary, and resolved to win further distinction. The article was an item in the darkened boyhood of his child.

A little log hut the size of a small room, chinked with mud; one fireplace (the kitchen); one bed, with knotted ropes for springs; one room; a chromo of a boxing match on the walls; a nest where the pet hen laid her eggs in the corner; a rat trap under the bed; some old trousers half filling the broken windowpane; rude boxes for chairs and hard dirt for a floor—such was Roy Keough's birthplace.

But there was a big apple tree less than three feet from the front door, with flowers as pink and white as Colonel Russell's, and a mocking bird sang nightly in the white pine near the spring. Having so little else pleasant to look upon, the South Mountain lad saw the humming bird weave her soft, warm nest, and at three years of age loved the wood thrush as many men love a dollar. The woods were wide and unneighbored, and fish were in the streams, and songs in the sweet-shrub scented air. He listened to voices that many die not having heard, and saw what the multitude, living, never see. True to his traditions, he grew up having no enemies save a revenue officer, and no contempt save for the neighbor who had bought a stove like the town folks. Shut in by the silent, sleepy mountains, Dunvegan (twelve miles) was far beyond heaven, and even ten-housed Glen Alpine was "town."

To sketch the visage of the South Mountains is to write about a beautiful woman's face, to try to say something more of a good man, to attempt to praise a pink-throated lily; it is the rude whisper in the midst of the symphony. A beautiful land, with all the witchery of forests and meadows and silver-ribboned streams—a land where the woods are spirit and the spirits are wood! In a cove where the sweet-breathed winds beat in upon the billowy green of shrub and tree the Keough cabin was hidden, betrayed only by the curling blue smoke from the mud-chinked chimney. Only the elements were there—the lightning one day, the blue daisy the next; the white snow to love in the winter, the pink-tongued kalmia to kiss all summer long.

Twelve miles away was Dunvegan, where men wore "biled shirts" and shiny shoes and shaved their necks; proud Dunvegan, where the women had no warts on their hands nor knew how to kill hogs nor cut their own fire wood; citified Dunvegan, where were fences before the houses and where people planted grass in their front yards! Even as a child Roy heard such curious things. Some day he would go there for himself and see. It would seem strange to look upon two-story houses and Dr. Wilfong's big church that would hold two hundred people and the steam engine! There Roy's imagination broke its wing.

Yet he went to Dunvegan and found the devilship of the *Democrat* as naturally as any flea finds its puppy. Colonel Russell, "editor and proprietor," taught him his "cases;" and when he had tarried in the print shop until his beard was almost grown, Dr. Wilfong (whose throne was in the little red church in under the oaks) declared that he was destined to be a great journalist, and wrote Henry Webster, who owned the Atlanta *Commonwealth* about it.

Because the Doctor said it, Dunvegan became too small for Roy, and he was called to the literary editorship of the *Commonwealth*. As he read his offer the thought flashed over him that he, a son of the South Mountains, might go, and come back to Dunvegan and be known among them as a gentleman. He went and trusted and worked and kept on seeing.

The thing that Roy Keough did in the great metropolis was a thing to do. There have been those who held high positions worthily; but their name is not legion who hold lesser ones as a king would wield his scepter. Unloved and fearfully the plebeian son of the South Mountains arrived at the notorious train shed. But it was noticeable that as he passed out into the street he straightened back his shoulders and tilted his chin to go forward; and the first thing he did was to say: "I love Atlanta." Life surged about him, and he looked at it, saw beauty in it, and from the rude jargon of noisy street rumblings he drew a song. It was a worthy thing in him that he called it an honor to be allowed to enter the great city, which drew dregs and genius for a radius of hundreds of miles. From the sooty window of his dingy little office in the *Commonwealth* Building he looked down upon the struggling thousands. It was as meaningful as the song of the mocker at midnight. This language that all things spoke — the confusion of tongues in the bickerings of the byways — it was his part to understand. He interpreted. He looked at men and animals and things, and loved them. He thought about them. His pen knew only the habit of writing kindly of them. The street happenings he treated tenderly, using invective and ridicule as a good surgeon would use his knife. In an utter abandon of love he gave away his heart to his pen. Long before they knew his face on the streets half the populace read the *Commonwealth* with scissors in hand. The Wa-haws became as well known as Stone Mountain. Other people learned to interpret the deeds of men as a language, watching happenings as the dumb watch the hands of one who would speak with them. All this thing did Roy Keough in the great city of Atlanta, where the average man is as well known as a leaf in the forest.

Nor was it a strange thing that this son of the South Mountains, who began life looking for beauty in a village, should have found Infinity in a city. Unconsciously others took him by the hand and joined with him in the search. When they found that he was an interpreter, they came to him confused by whisper and shouting. He became Atlanta's week-day pastor of the thousands who longed for an interpretation of things, a spiritualization of that which they saw could not be all material. He had come from the silences where men had time to listen, and the habit was strong upon him. In the land of his nativity God had made all things. How could he forget it? And this great city, with its myriads of lights in its mountainlike buildings, with its disquieted multitudes anxious as his native lilies were never anxious for to-morrow, with its unled thousands who were beginning to call all things common — O, that the infinite muteness of the Wa-haws might come upon them! Else how would they ever know the accents of the Voice?

CHAPTER II

"The End"

"The execution is almost perfect; but it is not the execution that is drawing the crowds to admire it," Henry Webster remarked to his young protégé.

"No?" the journalist queried.

"It is the new sociology, the sociology of the Third Race, depicted on the canvas, and, it must be confessed, rather cleverly. The woman is unquestionably a genius, and beautiful, very beautiful, though one hesitates to say it in Atlanta, where the 'one drop' might as well be a bucketful. Have you seen her?"

"No," Roy Keough admitted, with the regret of a reporter who has missed a "beat."

"Nor the painting? Then come with me. She has just gone away with Kongo Copelin, one of *my* professors, but the picture is still here."

The two men sauntered through the crowds who had come to attend the closing exercises of Webster University, past the little coteries of white men and women who would smile upon the commencement of the famous negro school, past the denser collections of colored students, until they stood before the painting that all Atlanta was talking of.

"'The End,'" Webster murmured. "Has she named it well, Keough?"

The painting was a large canvas, handsomely framed in gilt. It portrayed the doorway of a laborer, a white man, who, clad still in the clothing of toil, stood by the side of his wife, with his arm resting tenderly upon her shoulder. Into the face of this wife the artist had thrown all the charm of exquisite beauty, from the black, curly locks to the daintily penciled lips, which seemed too pure for sensuous touch. Her dark eyes looked fondly upon her husband, beside whom she stood in lissom grace. A little child, fair of face, played at their feet; and a woman—an octoroon, perhaps—smiled upon the trio from the shadows of the doorway as if she would bless her daughter and her grandchild, and the white man who was not ashamed of his own. Written all over the canvas was the heart prophecy of the artist as plainly as in the name itself.

" 'The End.' What say you, Keough? Has she named it well?"

"She has named it as well as any dream may be named," Keough said, thoughtfully. "The only thing that bothers me is—"

"That they are beginning to dream it?"

"No, no! Where did she get that face from?"

"The face of the woman in the picture?"

"Yes. It seems very beautiful. Is it her own?"

"Hardly. You would certainly not know one from having seen the other. Perhaps she dreamed it for her child."

"Did you say she was a negress, Mr. Webster?"

"The daughter of an octoroon, I understand. There are few brighter white men in the city than her father. Can you keep a secret?" he added, in a whisper.

"Have I ever betrayed one?"

"Lawson, the dentist."

"Dr. Lawson? Is it possible?"

"Hush! He is here. There he comes now."

The two men stood aside while Dr. Lawson approached. He passed quickly, merely giving the painting a glance. He was a tall, strongly built man, already gray, with the powers which had made him famous very plain upon him. Short as was his glance at the painting, Roy Keough saw in it something—a new thing which he had not heard in the silences of the Wa-haws. He saw that a white man could love his offspring whose mother was an octoroon; he saw, also, that he could be proud of her work.

"Dr. Lawson!" he exclaimed again, softly, when the celebrated dentist had passed.

"It was in his younger and wild-oat days," Webster explained. "You have heard before that he came of common stock."

"I have, indeed; but I did not know before how common it was. I should like to see the girl—"

"You can easily meet her."

"Did you notice that I said 'see her?'" Keough corrected, gently.

"By the way, Roy, she is to marry one of my professors, a comparatively negroid fellow from the black belt—Dr. Kongo Copelin."

"Really? I am more interested in her art; yet it seems a pity. She is really a white girl, as most of your students are, Mr. Webster."

"Do you know, Keough," the editor assented, "just between us, when I founded this college, I thought it was for negroes. Frankly, I have since come to believe that there are no negroes when it comes to education; it is for the Third Race—for those who are pushing to 'the end.'"

They stood studying the painting thoughtfully.

"Shall I notice it in the *Commonwealth*?" Keough asked, slowly.

"Something has already been said about it — too much, I believe. The *Press* called me a 'negrophile' because one of our reporters described the artist as one of Atlanta's most beautiful women. But apart from all such jokes, Keough, you should see her. I am as white a man as anybody, and yet I tell you I have never seen so beautiful a woman, except once, and that was very long ago."

Keough smiled knowingly. They both remembered that face in Dunvegan.

"It is never too late to return in such case," Keough suggested.

"No. Well, perhaps — perhaps I may before the evening comes; but let us return to the *Commonwealth* Building. I have some editorials to write."

They walked through the corridor of the main building on out upon the broad campus, the yellow faces of the students turning to gaze upon them as the magnet looks toward the pole. Henry Webster was in more than one sense their benefactor. Out of his abundant wealth he had built Webster University for them and aided in richly endowing it. Over it he continued to preside in a sort of Jovian way, taking scarcely less interest in it than in the *Commonwealth*, the great Georgia daily of which he was proprietor, and on which Roy Keough was the most popular reporter. It was, therefore, a matter of interest to him that a woman of such excellent parts as this Lola Lawson Johnson ("Lola L.," it was always signed) should have graduated at his school and have stirred Atlanta with her pretentious attempt at painting her dreams. To Roy

Keough the thing came in a different light. He was ever the interpreter. This was a new phase of a very deep subject; it needed to be thought about, to be understood; yet instinctively he dismissed it from his mind long before he reached his desk in the *Commonwealth* Building. If the shadow was to come upon him, it must at least await the bidding of Fate.

CHAPTER III

A Muddy-Footed Fairy

"So you think that at least I am but a muddy-footed fairy?" she asked, looking not unkindly at him.

"But a fairy ever," he rejoined. "And you must hear the defense of our people, Lola; simple fairness requires that."

The woman was indeed beautiful; and if any trace of the negroid clung to her, her appearance suggested none of it. Lithesomely built, with the certain movement and gentle springiness of health and the grace of the dance and the tennis racket upon her, she stood facing a negro under the shades of the great water oaks of Webster University campus. The black ringlets of her curls would not be bound by the red ribbon band, which, after all, was there only to complement them; and her features — there was a certain soft, symmetrical fullness about them which to all men would seem compelling. Her nose was so sensitively shaped that it seemed possessed of mind and heart. Kongo Copelin was looking down into her eyes to read his fortune there — eyes which seemed able to hold all others until they were done with them; brown eyes, whose brightness and cleverness he forgot for dreaming the dreams he saw in them. He himself was not an ill-looking man, had his skin not been of an ebony blackness; for his features, like those of the better African tribes, were as regular as a Caucasian's. He was tall and strong and stalwart, and his college training had made an athlete of him, who, had he labored upon the farm, would have been known as a "big buck nigger." He had stretched out his hand to touch her. The ineffable line-bred sadness of a thousand years, a thousand centuries, was in his face as she withdrew from him with a little start. Was it the whiteness in her that did it? She was, indeed, a white woman. But why should he not? Was not one of the nursery stories told oftenest in the Hausa that of how the gorilla and the orang-outang would come out of the jungle into the villages and carry away the women to their tree homes in the forest? They were strong. So, also, he was strong.

"You must hear my defense," he continued, "for I also am a negro, and I know them for their worst. Strong, smelly, wild animals some of the lowest of us seem, half tamed and subdued by a civilization which they fear, looking upon it as the first wolf looked at the fire circle of the men to whom they came in. These are among my race, with a hundred millenniums of forest shades distilled into the pigment of their skins. Men of the jungle, they are where only the black could live, for all lighter skins furnished targets for preying beasts and burning sun. They are dazed for a moment by the light of the fire circle. But wait; they will learn to understand — "

"Possibly, or possibly not; but it was not of that I was thinking," she interrupted.

"If I were unkind," he continued, with a slight show of feeling, "I could say: what have they in common with these insipidly chalky-faced people who hunted them down and brought them hither, and who play a different game entirely from that which their people had played at for ages in the Dark Continent? Do I wish to be one of them? Yes, and No. Yes, as a man would be like angels; no, as he would cry out for flesh and bone again. And you, Lola, your face is white and your cheeks pink, yet you are one of us."

The woman paled and shuddered.

" 'One of them,'" she murmured. "Listen, Kongo! What would you do? If not one-tenth part of your blood were negro, and that part not of an ignoble strain; if, when dissociated from negroes, men counted you white; if your training and ambitions and education all identified you with the White Circle, would you want to be called 'nigger?' Would you allow your life to be forced back among the jungle people?"

"Yet, already," he replied, sturdily, "that people have furnished America with poets and artists and educators and done half the heavy work of the continent. Could the white child of the neolithic age, suddenly transported into the twentieth century, have done more?"

"Why don't you go on?" she urged. "Why don't you call them 'types' and be quit of it? O, how sick I am of all this silly twaddle, with its pictures of octoroons and quadroons handed out as negroes by magazines that never can understand! And I, in whose blood is half the black measure of an octoroon—no doubt I am 'a type of the negro student at Webster University.' Have I no right of protest against being classed with the black-fellows? Have you no more discrimination than these Aryans show in attributing to the jungle people the success of the Third Race? Would you also reprobate me as a negro because there is 'one drop' in my veins?"

She paused a moment in the avalanche of her words. Once a famous leader of her people had come to Atlanta to speak to them. Men called him "a great man"—white men did so. How it had fired her people's imagination to think of it! By sheer force of superior manhood he had risen until he was called by a white rabbi, "the greatest Southern man, save Lee." Such a man had come to Atlanta, whither all men came, to speak to her people; and how he had stirred them! He called them *his* people, *his* race, *his* kindred. And yet, even then, a schoolgirl, she could see the pitiful pathos of it all, for they were not *his* people. Only by so much as a muddied foot did he partake of their clay. In every essential thing he was a white man, save his color, and even there he was far removed from the black faces he called "brethren." This was the pathos of his life, and of hers also. He might lead white men, wield white men, and know himself superior to white men, but his camp fire must be a separate one; she, too, had some one not whispered undreamed-of things in her ears. There was Dr. Lawson, the distinguished dentist, and Laura Lawson, his daughter, and Lola Lawson, whom few could distinguish from her full-white sister. Ah, the pathos of the 'one drop!'

"I could not accuse you," he said, slowly. "If it were incumbent upon me to arraign any one, I should save all my scorn for the white betrayer of your mother. It is no accusation to me to be called an 'African.'"

Africa! It was the name of Hannibal's city, and thence of the giant continent whose size was greater and whose civilization was older than these parvenu Americas. More than half a thousand years before the coming of the White Christ their Northern settlements had circumnavigated the continent, and in the valley of her Nile black and white and brown men had intermingled so long that the memory of history ran not to the contrary. And Hausaland, his patria! When America was being discovered, did not his grandparent rule almost as many subjects as there were people in the United States to-day? — his grandparent, whose will was done from the Benue to the blue Mediterranean; whose subjects were happy, civilized, industrious, and hospitable, when the new-rich continent was a howling wilderness. Yet he — Kongo, a prince of the Hausa blood — was accounted by these Aryans an outcast, a pariah, who dared not enter the circle of their home light for fear of a kick and a curse.

He was a black-fellow, with an education and a gentleman's soul; and this was his sociology.

"What right have they," he asked, as if it contained the gist of the whole matter, "to reverence Jehovah and laugh at Unkulunkulu?"

"The odor of the jungle, the smell of the undisturbed mold, and the touch of green, wet things still clings to them," she murmured.

"They *are* black-faced sons of the equator—I know it well," he admitted— "bred to color in the shadowed forests. They fit the darkness and feel for it as wrong searches for midnight. But will white men never learn that the black-fellow will not think the world in Aryan categories, that they will forever refuse to play the games the white-fellows play at? And why should they? You will have to take sides, Lola. Be one or the other in the clash of interests."

"There is no clash of interests."

"You are not aware, then, of the state of war that darkens the future of both races and asks: 'Which of them shall possess the land?'"

"I know of but one race of people on this continent who shall inherit the earth," she said, significantly.

"You mean the Aryans?"

"I do not."

"Then surely not the negro?"

"Nor the negro."

"Then you mean your Third Race—potentially, in the future."

"Exactly."

"But where is that wonderful Third Race?" he asked, bitterly. "It will not be."

"On the contrary," she added, with prophecy in her eyes. "It is here; it is I and my kind, and our name is 'Legion!'"

"Sixteen to one," he murmured, smiling. "Are we to be submerged in a flood of white corpuscles?"

"Have you seen 'The End?'" she asked.

"Yes," he replied, looking straight into her eyes; "and I am afraid of it."

"Afraid! Are you so proud of the black pigment?"

"No; afraid of you. You dreamed that painting, and the face of the hero was white. I feared it. Does it mean—?"

There was a long silence.

"You have not answered?" he queried, petulantly.

"Nor shall I," she replied, coloring. "May not a woman have her dreams? What if she claims the right to choose her own motifs?"

"So you are like the rest!" he cried, angrily. "One hope, one ambition—to be white. No, to seem white, to be a mother of half—"

He stopped suddenly.

"You almost went too far that time, Kongo, did you not?" she asked, smiling. "You forgot that I am what I am because a negro woman preferred a white father for her children."

The black gentleman rose to his full height in unconscious courage.

"You are wrong!" he cried, passionately. "Say, rather, because a blackleg chose your mother to betray her!"

"Why should I not flock with my own?" she added, not noticing his arraignment. "You have told me I was the most beautiful woman in Atlanta. So have others. White men are continually raising their hats to me by mistake. If there were none to rise up against me and bear witness, I could be a white matron to-morrow. But notice, Kongo, I said 'matron,' not 'mistress.' In the beginning of the process our women must needs be the latter. But for me the process is over. I am ready now for the former."

His look was dark, as of envy clouded with anger at the unblushing confession of it.

"It has always been so with my people," he said, bitterly. "Through the trackless jungles for millenniums they have gone single file. No union, no strength, no power of combined efforts — only geese on their way down the path."

"Listen, Kongo," she replied, embittered. "You are a teacher in Israel, and yet you cannot understand. Cannot you see why? If the truth were known, who could deny that they were once as black as you are, or you as white as they? Whatever the primitive color, their ancestors went north to the cool, moist forests of Germany and bleached their skin and hair. Ours went south to the burning heat of equatorial Africa and burned the black in for centuries. Perhaps only the black ones among us could live where any show of color brought on us a hundred preying beasts; perhaps only dark skins survived the glare of a torrid sun; perhaps that sun, little by little, burnt the color into us. Certain it was that the fittest survived in tropical Africa, and the fittest will survive in subtropical America. Follow the equator around the world, Kongo, and for hundreds of miles north and south of it what do you see? Dark-skinned peoples. From Rome to Nyanza it is so; from the Himalayas to Madagascar. Is subtropical America to be the exception? The people who lived on this continent before the white folk came had dark skins and black hair and black eyes. Why? 'Adaptive coloration' you professors call it, and it is unquestionably so. What, then, of these white people? Was that why their God brought us here to infuse into their blood the power to live where the summer temperature seeks a hundred degrees as a companion? They despise us. Is their punishment to be the blackening of their breed?"

"O, Lola!" he cried, passionately, "you talk now as you used to do when you welcomed my embraces. Tell me—"

"Hush! Don't speak beside the mark," she continued, quickly. "They talk of the negro as if they feared his dominion, and yet they are the scientific race. Do they not know that the fittest survive? I read their books, their poems, their songs, and the tragedies they weep over. But, O holy Jesus, this is the tragedy none write about nor care for!"

She almost gasped out the words, and then grasping his arm and pointing a shaking finger at two girls passing under the arc light, she continued:

"Look at them! One as black as a Bantu princess, and

the other as white as I am. O, can't you see it! Can't anybody see it? She is a castaway white girl, a negro to her own, a suspect to the black folk. *Look on her and you see the Tragedia Americana, the horror of the one drop!*"

"The horror that grows and grows until all are to be partakers of it," he continued for her, sarcastically. "Surely it is a subject for the great American novel."

"The great American novel!" she exclaimed. "There will be no great American novel until there is a great American race. The Aryan tales of to-day are no more to be classed as American than the songs of the Welsh bards are representative British productions. That is why it will be centuries before the great American novel is written; and when it is written, negro blood will help write it."

"And yet, Lola," he cried, softly, "you have refused me my kiss three times this night. Can't we love one another? Why may we not?"

"Listen, Kongo, and I will tell you why we may not," she answered, excitedly. "Look at that negro over there! He looks like I've always imagined a Hottentot would look. He has on a Knox hat, clean collar, tailored clothes, and tan shoes. He is dressed up for the commencement occasion as if he were going over to Darktown to run with his girl. Yet, look at him! He's a chimpanzee. See his monkey face, his sensual features, his plaintive, baffled-brute look, as if a wild beast who is living among things he cannot understand. See his kinky wool and thick, padded lips. Do you think I want my children to look like him? Why should they not have brown hair and blue eyes?"

The man leaned back heavily against the oak. Here, indeed, was a brutality of statement and a scorn of racial pride and virtue. What white man would have said it?

27

"I am sorry, Kongo," she continued, "that our love affairs have been transformed into a discussion of ethnology. Perhaps 'The End' did have something to do with my change of feelings. One never is able to stop when one begins dreaming. But, after all, Kongo, what a useless thing it is for a race to kick against the pricks, even the white race! The mother continent which they have called "America" after one of their own number knows no love for white faces. Her children have been tall and dark-skinned, tawny and high of cheek bone. The eternal gifts she has given them made them so—her sun, her soil, her mothered foods, her maize, her meats. Will a mother change the hue of her children? No. Dark they were, black-eyed and black-haired, and dark they will remain. Already keen observers are noting the change—how the whites are taking on the physical characteristics the mother continent requires of her children. Wait until they have blended into an octoroon nation, and even Sitting Bull would think their breed his."

But the man said nothing more.

"He is indeed brave," she added, more gently, "who lays his plans without thought of mother continent. Whoever and whatever lives upon her back does not so of its own accord, but because she wills it so. Africa loved the zebra and hippopotamus and negro, and made them for herself. Bright-faced America chose the red man and the turkey. Destroy her fauna, and she merely goes to work to create them again. That is why the race inhabiting this continent will always be dark, and he who lives along the Niger black. Asia loves yellow and Europe loves white, just as you, Kongo, love—"

She turned to look upon him, perhaps to ease his pain with a touch; but he had gone.

Gathering her skirts gracefully, she walked swiftly to her dormitory—she, the white woman who would not be a negro, the negro who could not be white. As she passed under the trees, two gentlemen went by the arc light.

"It is Mr. Webster and Mr. Keough," she murmured. "Both of them are handsome, and neither is married. I wonder what they thought of 'The End.'"

CHAPTER IV

THE BEGINNING OF THE END

The soft haze of the Indian summer covered the rolling foothills of the Blue Ridge with a mystic veil which Roy Keough loved to gaze upon. From his window on the fourteenth floor of the *Commonwealth* Building he looked out upon it and watched the dreamy mist slowly obscure the distant hills. The lights of the great city gleamed below him, and the elevators in the skyscrapers around winked at him as they passed from floor to floor. The crowds grew denser at Silverman's Corner till the women were holding to the straps on the street cars. The searchlights of the motor cars blinded the stranger at the crossings and made him pause to practice his eyesight on the giant structures rising to fabulous heights around him and wonder at the dæmon of Atlanta. "O, magic name!" thought Keough, looking out upon the panorama before him; Atlanta, the fleet-footed maiden who had outstripped all comers to the race, even though she had stooped to grasp the golden apples of Hippomenes by the way! Wonderful city, whose love had made men great, whose spirit breathed the Eternal Urge into her children! From the corners of the earth she had drawn her own together to race with her for the attainment of great things. "My spirit shall be the prize of all who run with me in the race, and death the penalty of those who try and fail." Thus she spoke to those who breathed her breath after her, who came from afar to seek her hand with no apples of gold to aid them in the race. The spirit of that which is to come was hers, of the farther plan waiting to be born. The creators of the earth had heard of her, and come hastily to join in making things. Their blood, their blazonry, their history—these things mattered not; but the questions were: Had she placed the Eternal Urge within them? Could they make a thing? Could they dream that which was to be? Could they strive for her hand? Would they stake their all upon the issue and seek out their Venus on her Cyprian isle to pray for their apples?

"O, mighty city!" he murmured, softly, "I love you, love you! We will run the race together. Breathe thou the spirit of thy glorious haste into my nostrils!"

It had grown darker when he walked out upon the pavement of Peachtree Street and turned northward toward his home. He would take a brisk walk to his lodgings. As he passed through the crowds at Silverman's Corner, the Fates reached out their hands to take him.

The Third-Race woman came rapidly down the street toward him. In a sort of subconscious way he recognized her as Laura Lawson, and wondered why she had come back from her New York trip so soon. Automatically he reached for his notebook, for it must be in to-morrow's "Personals." Before he could more than touch his pencil, a sudden turn of the current of foot passengers threw them opposite one another; in fact, she almost ran into his arms. He had met her once at a church reception, but she would probably not recognize him. Instinctively he raised his hat, and said: "I beg a thousand pardons, Miss Lawson!"

"Pardon *me*, Mr. Keough," she answered, amused at his expression of regret. "Really in Atlanta we seem to be compelled to throw ourselves at people!"

Lola Lawson started thus upon her long-dreamed madness, for she knew she had been mistaken for her full-white half-sister.

He was pleased, and she was beautiful. New York had dealt kindly with her.

"It was my fault entirely," he apologized. "Absent-minded—"

"You need no explanation." Her heart pounded her bosom for that he had not recognized her, and it had grown a custom with her of late to drink of these white nectars on the streets. "But I wonder what thought could have been so pleasant as to make you forget that you were at Silverman's Corner."

"Would you really care to know, Miss Lawson?"

Then she understood, and her heart beat fast. He had admired her sister.

"Should I? Who would not wish to know even one paragraph of the 'Song and Story' before it appears in the *Commonwealth*?"

"You are a splendid guesser, so far as the *Commonwealth* is concerned; but it was not a song, and certainly not a story. I was reaching for this pencil to make note that you were an Atlantian again."

"Again? I am always."

"Then you will certainly take a coca-cola with me."

"And put antikink on this hair to take these curls away?" she bantered, fighting for time to think.

"Not by the antikink man's fortune, all of which he would give for one of those ringlets. But you may say what you please about the post-office receipts. Is it Chicago we passed with the current year ending—"

"And of Peachtree Street?"

"Yes, your native—but perhaps you were not born here."

"Born here!" she exclaimed, laughing. "Have you ever heard of any one who was born in Atlanta?"

"Come!" he said, catching some of her hilarity. "You have the spirit, and it is only a few steps to the Crystal Palace."

Why should she not? One day by mistake in the Scanlon Building she had absent-mindedly failed to take the elevator marked "For Boxes, Trunks, and Negroes," and had entered that "For Whites Only." Yet half a dozen men had politely lifted their hats, and more than one of them looked at her with manifest admiration.

"If I go to my doom, it will be God's palaver," she muttered, lowering her veil and taking her place by his side.

By that strange law of subconscious association of ideas she suddenly found herself asking of herself: "What became of the ancient Roman slaves whose skins were black?"

"It would take centuries—centuries to assimilate them," she seemed to hear Kongo Copelin say.

"There is no lack of centuries," she had replied.

CHAPTER V

A Window in Atlanta

Kongo Copelin remembered her words as he walked slowly down the street.

"And you want me to do a thing," she had said, "that no Third-Race girl of my class would do. Do you not know that fewer and fewer quadroon girls are willing for their families to grow any darker?"

It was, indeed, a bitter thing. "Black fellow, tumble down; jump up, white fellow," was a saying he had heard among his people; and his father had told him of how a friend, who had been smuggled to America a few years before the war, had thrown himself into the Chattahoochee one night, hoping to awake among his people on the tangled banks of the Benue. "What a curious craving they must have to be white!" he muttered.

There had been a day long ago on the slave coast when the simple black folk, to whom transmigration was an eternal verity, supposed these strange ethereal beings who came among them from Europe to be their own dead who had come back to them from the other world for the love wherewith they had loved their country. But now—

"Yet why are these pale people great?" he thought. "Is it not because in the frozen North it was only the fittest who survived, and the fittest were the greatest in brain as well

as in brawn? And why are we black people their servants?"
he added. "Because of an equatorial, enervating sun and
a climate that served our meals regularly on the trees.
Their snow and cold and wind made them great, and it
will make us great also — given time — centuries; and she
says there is no lack of centuries."

But she had called his people "chimpanzees!"

As he was thinking thus, he remembered, revengefully,
how the chimpanzee and the white man were associated
in the minds of the forest folk in his native Africa, the pale
yellow of the former serving to resemble the Aryans.

So he mused on.

"Why should these Teutons wonder at that animal look
of untamable wildness in their faces? For a thousand generations their brother had been old saber-tooth and their
mortal foe the lion. They had learned to fear and be silent, and the fear that must speak had found expression
in their eyes. These loud-tongued Aryans who babbled
all they knew, who seemed never to keep their words off
their tongues — no wonder they could not understand
the instinctive secretiveness of the savage. As to his own
people, it would take a dozen centuries to drive the forest wildness from their eyes, to remove the smell of the
jungle from them. They were men at least, for they had
not gone backward. Any Bantu child could tell the curious legend of the monkey-men — apes, who used to be
men, but took to living in the forests with the tree people.
Compare this with the unparalleled record of his race
in America during the last forty years. And all this talk
about the assaulting of white women! See how these phallic whites betrayed the black women, and no one noticed
it at all. And the more he thought of the cruel duplicity

of the white deal, the more his wrath was stirred. These Caucasian men who with one voice proclaimed themselves poor worms of the dust and with the next promised each other that they were to be the sons of God, a white God—willing enough to rise from a dunghill to a palace, but unwilling that a black-faced brother should enter their circle—what would God say of them if perchance he should prove a black God, if his name should be Unkulunkulu instead of Jehovah?"

"Halala!" he exclaimed, using the Zulu cry of exultation. "Then they would have their reward."

As he spoke, he came opposite the white splendor of the Crystal Palace. He looked in at the glistening tiling and the mirrors resplendent with light. The brilliant glow of it held his eye, and he paused for a moment on his way.

"Becalmed and looking at the fish," he murmured, remembering the African proverb of the poor man who gazed wistfully at what he might not grasp.

A woman and her escort brushed by him and entered the white splendor beyond. Kongo moved obsequiously aside.

"Behind dog it is dog," he muttered, "but before dog it is Mr. Dog!"

"Neither ape nor man are we," he continued, bitterly. "There is scarce a child in West Africa who does not know that apes are really wiser than negroes, for they had sense enough to keep their mouths shut, so that they would not have to work! But the wonder—"

There he stopped, for the face seemed strangely familiar despite the veil, which was drawn down as far as its owner chose. She sat with her friend at a table partly separated from the rest, and she herself faced Peachtree. His back was thus to the street, and only were he to turn could he be recognized. This had not happened, but the girl was frequently looking rather furtively toward the door. The eyes that thrilled men till they came to their knees, the nose so delicately penciled, the dark curls—all these—were—they—not—his? She lifted her face; the electric light suddenly fell full upon it.

"Lola Lawson!" he exclaimed, excitedly. "It is she, or I am crazy!"

A man passing by, who had been gazing as all the rest toward the effulgence beyond, turned to look at him, and, seeing that he was a negro, passed on.

"She has fled from the sword and hid in the scabbard," he muttered. "She would be burned at the stake if they discovered her. He thinks it is her sister. Who—can—he—be?"

He watched them then as they sat under the brilliant lights. The Crystal Palace was one glow of effulgence, and gay enough even for a girl who knew herself to be drinking madness with her frappé. The muffled feet of young white boys flew here and there as they sped to fulfill the orders of the guests. Mr. Webster, the richest man in Atlanta, was there with Dr. Wilfong, his friend from Dunvegan, and more than one of the upper tier sat round their gossipy tables. Lola Lawson scarcely once turned her face from the Peachtree way, so that he could see her every expression, and the man faced her at the table. In spite of the warping fire of his jealousy, Copelin felt that they were mates far more than he and the white-black girl could ever be. The man was handsome and well groomed and vivacious enough, and of the pair seemed to be enjoying himself the more. The girl's finely chiseled lips seemed sometimes to quiver a little with fear—the fear of the animal of the wild who was lost from her people and has found them again. It was, perhaps, fear lest such as he, Kongo, might come in and claim her as a renegade—come in and say: "You belong to the black people. The taint of our blood is in your veins. You are a jungle woman. You have forsaken your kind for the White Circle. You—" Then the man, the Teuton, would drive her back into the jungle again. For a moment Kongo was tempted to do just this thing. What right had she to leave him? He was the son of a king of the jungle; she, a daughter of plebeians, in spite of her wonderful beauty. Then he remembered that she was now within the Circle, that with her eyebrows she could destroy him, and the man in all probability shoot him down on the tiled floor as the fire people used to do to the tree folk who came too near. No; but he would watch the perfidy of it.

The man loved her; he could see it by his tones, his gestures, his bearing. She could see it, too, yet she seemed to be afraid of something. The man whispered eagerly and said something, before which he measured the nearness of his neighbors with a hasty glance. She had blushed and risen to go, but the man put out his hand and touched her, and she sat down again. He could hardly believe it was Lola. As the man had half risen he had partly turned his face, and the features, half seen, seemed remarkably familiar. He was handsome, and bore himself with the manners of a Southern gentleman, and the girl seemed already dear to him. Yet he was probably of no more ancient family than Kongo; and had he been in the class of '01, he would probably have scarce outranked others whom the black professor had beaten. What right had he to take the girl away? And what did he want with her? He was not so strong as Kongo, nor more of a gentleman bred. Did the glow of the fire circle make his halo for him? And should the lineal descendant of Ubamba, the king, let this European serf steal his woman away because the black man learned last to build his camp fire? No! By all the terrors of the jungle, he would go into that room if he were shot down the next moment, and tell the man that he should not have her! He would—

The man had risen, and the white light shone full upon his features.

It was Roy Keough!

Kongo moved back into the shadows of the gutter. The white man and the woman who would come out of the forest to sit by his fire circle passed him quickly. The man looked out to the streets and said to his companion, who had lowered her veil:

"Did you see that negro there to the left? His face reminded me of a wild beast's glare."

"And do you know," she replied, as he took her arm and adjusted her wrap gently, "he has been gazing into the window for an hour?"

"Strange, isn't it?" he murmured. "They have but one ambition—to come in to the camp fire."

CHAPTER VI

The Dentist's Doorway

"See," said Keough, gayly, as they walked on out Peachtree, "here we are at the Scanlon Building. These roses in the florist's windows are not quite beautiful enough for your hands, but may we take them to your home? Come, let's go in for a bouquet. I didn't suppose Atlanta could furnish such beauties," he continued.

"Perhaps they are some that the Charleston papers are always throwing at our city," she suggested, gayly.

A look of amused appreciation was her reward for the sally.

"So you really read the *Commonwealth*?" he ventured.

"Read it? I know Dunvegan by heart; and as for Dr. Wilfong, by the way, was he the man who was afraid to wash the top of his buggy for fear of starting the village gossips?"

"Don't let's talk of Dunvegan to-night. It reminds me that for twelve years I have been wanting to go back there. I may never live in the sight of the Wa-haws, but at least this can be said of me Miss Lawson — that while others stay in Dunvegan and grow tired of her, esteeming the ill-kept, sunless city above their open spaces of sky and greensward, I, living where they would that they were, wish myself for nothing more than they have; nor do I ever forget the sunlit window of my boyhood home, nor the red-faced woodbine that clambered over the old white-washed fence. Do you know, Miss Lawson, I believe these are my eternal loves. They call me when I dine at the Attacoa or lunch in the New York Café. They say to me: 'We love only you; we know you dream of us nightly. We see your people daily and watch the spots you used most to love. We wait, fearing to die, lest possibly to-morrow you might come to find us gone.'"

As he said the last words he looked into her eyes, and it seemed to him that some miniature god of showers had cast his rainbows therein to be mended. The clerk was boxing the roses behind the counter to the rear; and the telltale moisture in her eyes and the entrancing odors of the flowers—

"Miss Lawson," he said, "I have planned to go back there some day, but I am afraid no one from Atlanta would go with me."

Her heart throbbed, and she knew her face was crimson. This was the white nectar she craved so. Ah, to drink it, drink it, drink it!

"'Miss Lawson?'" she whispered, softly.

He understood.

"Laura," he murmured, "you make me very happy."

"Few women are so blessed. You must tell me more of Dunvegan sometimes when this horrid clerk will stay away. See, he has finished his tying already."

Out into the night they went again—into the night turned day with a thousand brilliant lights.

"Let us walk slowly," she suggested. "I hate to rush."

"Your servant also. To hurry in Dunvegan was a crime. One might miss something; and I am sure I would to-night."

"That was good of you; and should my father be on the porch, it might be very true. Don't be alarmed if he orders me out of his house," she said, laughing.

But the awful tragedy of his possible presence made her tremble.

"Why doesn't he buy some watch-dogs and be done with it? Does he expect to keep you for himself?"

"I am afraid he is too considerate of you boys. But, seriously, I shall have to tell you good-by at the front gate."

"Then let me remind you of your prejudice; we are fairly rushing along."

She laughed softly.

"You are as refreshing as—what shall I say?"

"'A coca-cola,' of course. Where were you raised?"

"In Birmingham, where they cry, 'Come on; let's get drunk and tell our sho' 'nuff names!'" she exclaimed, laughing. "Why not as an automobile ride?"

"Because there are autos and autos. Now if it were in your father's—" he bantered.

"Then in my father's it shall be—his six-cylindered!"

"I was only joking—"

"But I was not. Besides, for shame to flout my invitation—"

"Laura!"

"Forgive me. I shall call for you at my convenience. But see, we are here at the gate."

It was before one of the older homes of Atlanta that they stood, built by a gentleman of another generation, and bought by the popular and successful dentist, whose accomplished daughter was in New York, and whose child of the demi-monde had now come, by a singular road—forced to tremble at the gate, lest her part in the drama should fail. The lights of the city street showed the white pillars before the doorway and lit up the perfect outline of it. The door was partly open, and within the form of a strong and commanding figure could be plainly seen.

But the gate was in the shadow of the magnolias, and he had not seen the girl enter. Nor was there any needless noise to disturb them. She stood gracefully leaning on the post from within, and Keough upon the gate from without.

"You must go now," she whispered, softly; "but we shall meet again. Good-by!"

"And will it be 'Laura' next time, too," he asked, "or will you forget what has passed?"

"Forget it?" she almost cried. "Would you think me foolish if I said—if I told—"

"Quick, please! Say on."

"That I could never forget it," she added, simply, leaning forward slightly toward him.

The figure in the doorway moved—came out and stood upon the porch.

"Please, Roy—Mr. Keough," she whispered, excitedly, "don't move, don't say a word, even if he speaks to us. He—he is almost insane if a young man comes home with me. Hush!"

Motionless they stood together in the shadows, and he reached out his arm to protect her. It was unconsciously done, for he was thinking of the new man who stood in the ancient doorway; but she leaned gladly upon it. The throb of his heart as he touched her! Surely she heard it, for she quivered and turned her face up toward him. In her eyes he read a lovely thing; and it was very dark under the magnolias. He leaned forward to touch her lips, and she smiled at him.

"Wait a little while," she murmured. "It will seem a very long one—to me."

But O, what a cup!—what a golden chalice to dash from her lips!

The figure still stood upon the porch, and the light from the open doorway behind him cast his shadow down the walk to the gate. He seemed to be looking for some one. But the man and woman at the gate made no movement. The man had come inside the gate, and the woman rested her head upon his shoulder. Keough watched the figure, and, since he must be quiet, he studied its meaning. On him the contrast was not lost. There was the ancient doorway, in which he seemed to see the pillars of the stout hearts who built and loved them, and the strong lintels of that civilization which prided itself upon its untarnished blood. Any one to whom the gods had given gold might go and buy one of these old-timy portals and look up at the entablature as if it were his. Architrave and frieze and cornice—he could tell the names and describe the mode of each. But if he be not to the manner born, how they mock him! The souls of pure, strong men are in them. For a man of mongrel stock, a seducer of the women of a child race, to walk in and out beneath those lintels is desecration indeed. The spirits of the long dead expressed themselves in those doorways. All their simplicity and elegance and strength is there, and the sons of the dado and gingerbread ornaments must not stoop to look into this ark, lest fire should come forth and consume them. There are things there which only those may see who also love. Ah, ye ancient doorways, blessed is the man who can pass through you and on to the path of his fathers and not notice the shortness of his stature!

Suddenly the man of the new era began walking down the steps of his house, and came on quickly toward the gate.

"I shall have to go on into the house," she said. "Get back into the shadows! Hush! Not a whisper!"

She came out then into the dim light which came from the open doorway.

"Why, child," Dr. Lawson exclaimed, starting suddenly at the sight of the daughter, "you frightened me! What are you doing here alone?"

She walked forward to meet him.

"Father," Keough could hear, "may I not sometimes —?" and then her words died out as they two passed on-ward into the house.

CHAPTER VII

Also a Teuton?

"Me git married? No, suh! Sallie I come, an' Sallie I'se gwinter go! Fo' chillun—fo' diff'unt white men; an' I ain't ashamed of it! You may call it 'crim'nal,' but the white men don't! I tells all my gals to do like their mammy an' they won't go far wrong."

Kongo Copelin looked at this mulatto woman, who had the unblushing hardihood to say such a thing, with a great sadness. It was infinitely repugnant, not only to his sense of decency, but of race destiny as well. Furthermore, it came from *her* mother.

Lola Lawson smiled at him amusedly.

"Mammy's philosophy is crude, isn't it? But see how time has tested it out. 'By their fruits ye shall know them.' Look on me!"

The octoroon woman spoke again, sharply.

"I know what you're a-thinkin', Copelin; but as for me, I'd a long sight rather be a white man's mistress than a nigger man's wife. I means for my chillun to have some sort o' show in life; an' I'se done learned early dat de brighter de face, de brighter de chance. Look at that gal o' mine there! You been teasin' her 'bout what she done t'other night at that Crystal Palace. You're ashamed of it. I glories in it, an' I prays God to let her git him; an' I ain't standin' in her way—not if dis co't knows itself."

The negro professor turned to Lola Lawson.

"Come," he said, "we must be going!"

They left the cheap cottage on Jackson Row and walked slowly toward the cleaner quarters of the city.

"Which way shall we stroll to-night?" he asked.

"Peachtree Street," she replied, lowering her veil.

"You want to say something to me," she began, falteringly. "Why did you stare at me so hard through the window?"

He was silent for a moment.

"Tell me," she urged. "Say it all; we are alone."

"Alone!" he answered, bitterly, musing as if half dreaming—"I and my fathers. It has ever been so! Alone on their vast continent they lived, gregarious rather than social, sons of the glorious jungle; kinsmen of the wild breeds therein, fleet as the hartebeest, thick-headed as the ostrich, adaptively colored as the zebra. Myriads of animals shared their valleys and velts, yet they lived alone among them, attaching none to themselves, domesticating no living thing, linking no single other creature permanently to the human race. How shall we be expected to adapt ourselves to this new world into which they who hunted us down have cast us? If for ages among a wonderful wealth of wild life we attached no single animated thing to us, how may we now excel in a world where a horse and his master have been buried together from time immemorial, where even the cats have hospitals? Tell me, Lola! I am alone. It is in the breed, is it not? That is why you are casting me off."

"I have not cast you off. I may fail—"

"And yet," he continued, "give us time, and men will forget our origin. They sit at their pianos daily, and none remember the rude huntsman's bow with its gourd resonator twanged around the camp fire, though the one is the child of the other—"

"Listen, Kongo!" she interrupted. "You mistake me. I also am a negro to the world. I love the negro race and admire it. What other people has so great a capacity for hard and unremitting labor—for humble, uncomplaining toil? Their weakness is their power. Of such are they who shall inherit the earth. But, Kongo, you have centuries of slow, painful evolution before you—I mean your race—before you shall be where the Aryan is now. That is what mammy meant. I am ahead of you— them—by a millennium. I—"

"Scarcely so long," he commented. "It did not take so many years for the despised Saxons to make their conquerors speak in their tongue."

"Suppose it were only a hundred years, Kongo; why should I go backward? But I am now where the whole black race will not be for a millennium."

"A millennium!" he replied, slowly. "Ten centuries only? And there is no lack of centuries? I pray God it may be a thousand millenniums before the whole black race is where you are!"

She winced. After all, there was something magnificent about this coal-black fellow.

They stood thoughtfully now before an Aryan home far out Peachtree Street. He looked backward to where the great city lay in the distance; she, upward into the summer sky. Her eyes were fixed on one of the stars which seemed larger than many of its companions, and very red and fiery. Her lips twitched as she gazed at it there a long while in silence. Then she reached forth her hand and touched him lightly.

"See!" she whispered. "Its pitiful, terrible redness tells the story. You asked me once to prophesy where your race would be a thousand years from now. A thousand years—it is but to-morrow! Yonder in the sky is a planet which has grown old during the past eternity. For the most part it is now a glaring, desert waste. Its inhabitants are in a last death grapple with the untamed forces which will surely end their civilization before many millenniums. Water almost gone; atmosphere attenuated; forests, waterfalls, rivers, seas—their children of to-day speak of these things as ours do of the Paleozoic Age, of far-past Devonian times. How many races do you suppose there are on Mars? Just as many as there shall be on this earth when its lowest ocean beds shall have become the last strongholds of a perishing civilization—one; just as many as there will be on this earth before we shall have to begin to cut canals to irrigate our ancient sea bottoms with the water from melted polar snows—one. And why not? Why should there not be a restoration of the primal man? Darwin crossed a Silky and a Black Spanish, and there came forth a jungle fowl, the primitive type. Why not with men?"

He laughed bitterly.

"Why not?" she urged. "The world is round. All things go here in circles."

"You do not understand the philosophy of their ethnology, Lola," he argued, thoughtfully. "There is no such thing possible now, they say. Race development and consequent variation have gone too far. One cannot obtain an amphibian by mating a fish and a bird, though they be children of common ancestors. Besides—forgive me, but you introduced the subject—you should know the

49

fatal physiological law that will sooner or later destroy your plans utterly, the law of the diminishing fertility of the — Third Race. If they would long perpetuate their kind, they must breed back to the black fellow or the white folk. You know, also, how the Indian of Mexico is breeding out the Spanish blood, which was alien to it, and slowly reverting to the American type. These things I am telling you are laws, they say — the fiats of Nature, who would hold her own in the development of the highest race types. There will be no *permanent* Third Race. The substratum isn't there. America will be black or white. My own opinion is that where the Aryan can live, it will be white; where he passes his climatic zone into the negro's latitude, it will be black. It will be a question of the will of the land — "Mother Earth," you call it. She alone has the right to choose between black and white father for her children.

"Almost," she murmured, "thou persuadest — you are a noble fellow, Kongo. If it wouldn't seem so absurd, I should like to say, 'God bless you!'"

"But, Lola," he urged, tenderly, "we want you; they despise you. I love you, a real woman; he fancies you are another woman. I will protect you, cherish you forever; he will cast you off — "

"Cast me off!" she exclaimed, quivering from head to foot. "Yes, now; but not after — after we are m — "

"Yes, after that — after anything. I tell it to you. It is in his blood. The Teutons have ever called their children by the bondwoman only *progeny*!"

"Even if — if he did," she murmured; "am I not also a — Teuton?"

CHAPTER VIII

Another Journalist Arrives

"Mr. Keough, shake hands with Mr. Elliston, of the *Modern Trend*. Mr. Elliston is down South for a little study of the negro problem at first-hand to give to his Northern constituency. Do you think you could find time, Roy, to show him Darktown and Jackson Row?"

"Certainly, Mr. Webster, if it is your wish," Keough replied, readily. "How long will you be down, Mr. Elliston?"

"Why, I wanted to get back day after to-morrow if I could. You see, I have been writing this series of articles on the 'Rights of the Colored Man,' and it occurred to me last week that a trip South might help them along — local color and all that, you know. So I remembered Henry here — we were college mates at Harvard — and just made up my mind to put a whole day in among them. By the way, I notice yours are very much blacker than ours. Is it the climate, do you suppose?"

Roy smiled. Webster grinned aloud.

"Really, I should have kept better posted on what was appearing in the *Trend*," Roy answered. "I know that series will be interesting. But as to the color of your Northern negroes, I believe it is a slight difference in blood. Ours are largely pure. You have to come South for the real thing in negroes. Don't you think so, Mr. Webster?"

"I was just telling Elliston that when you came in," Mr.

Webster replied. "Also, I suggested an automobile ride as the best way to learn their inner souls and see them in their home," he continued, with a laugh and a wink. "He was saying how much he had learned about their domestic habits already from the Pullman window. You see, in an auto you could go right down to their homes, give them a quarter, and tell them to talk."

"He would see the domesticated ones in that way, at the very least," Roy suggested.

"But the negro wild beast!" Webster added, with a tinge of irony, as if to emphasize his words.

An employee entered his office and handed him a telegram. Webster's features set hard and his fists clinched.

"My God, Elliston, I wish you fellows up New York way had something like this once a day on your desk to hash up for your readers! Listen here:

"Mary Morris, fourteen-year-old daughter of H. L. Morris, one of the most prominent business men of Atlanta, and Lucy Morris, her aunt, of twenty-five years of age, were criminally assaulted in the outskirts of the city early this morning. Miss Lucy Morris, with her young niece, was picking flowers in the woods in sight of near-by homes, and had no fear, since it was in broad daylight. With their hands full of ferns and flowers, they were returning along an old Confederate breastworks, when a negro met them, having a huge club in one hand and a large rock in the other. He struck down the fourteen-year-old girl, leaving her supposedly senseless, and then yelled at Miss Morris. In a few moments Mary revived and found herself bound to a tree. The negro stood over her.

" 'Honey,' he said, 'I want you to come with me. I'll be kind to you; you know I won't hurt you — '

" 'I can't,' Mary answered; 'my leg is broken;' and she let it hang limp to the ground.

"The negro grinned and went back to her aunt. Mary chose her chance, and, unbinding herself, ran, screaming for help. At this the negro fled. Mr. Morris arrived shortly. He found his sister lying with her face half buried in the sand. All the back of her head was beaten sore and bloody. The wild beast had slit the bridge of her nose wide open and had gouged one eye out of the socket. Mr. Morris is a well-known Atlanta business man, and his sister and daughter have many friends in the city."

"Now, Arthur Elliston," Webster continued, handing the paper to the visitor, "take that back with you to New York. That is enough to explain to my friends why I am Southern in my sentiments on this question from A to iz-zard. Take that back with you and write a chapter in your series on it. O, if you only had a few like that in New York, all the Manhattan police couldn't hold back the mob, nor the waters of the Hudson extinguish the torches!"

As he finished speaking, the shrill voice of a newsboy came from the street below:

"Here's your *Commonwealth*! Here's your *Evening Press*! Paper, mister? All about the new assault! Paper, mister?"

"Do you hear that cry, Elliston?" Webster continued. "I have heard it every week almost for months. It's beginning to get on my nerves. I've got a sister who stays alone with the servants all day long in my home; and, by the Eternal, if they touch her, I'll blow up Webster University!" His pale-blue eyes were afire. "And yet I have half an idea that it's just a sort of—Nemesis."

"Nemesis?" Elliston asked.

"Ah, boys, I haven't said it before, but, by the Eternal, *what respect for our women can you expect from another race whose women our blacklegs deflowered so d—— shamelessly?* What did they know of virtue when we brought them here, and who, in God's name, should have taught them?"

An office boy entered with some uncorrected proof. Webster glanced at it and saw his editorial matter for the evening edition. A double-leaded leader stood out boldly under its black title letters:

"CLEAN OUT THE DIVES! CLOSE UP THE SALOONS! THE PRESENT CRISIS CANNOT LAST MUCH LONGER! ABOVE ALL, KEEP COOL!"

"Those are my sentiments, Elliston," he continued. "I didn't add, 'Shoot down the wild beast at sight.' I hope to my God I will never say it. I hope we will never come in this country to burning their dens out as you do in the North. But what about your automobile ride? If you go in the right direction, you may see a lynching."

The office boy came back bearing a card in his hand, and gave it to Roy Keough.

"The lady says she will wait for you in her automobile."

Keough took up the card and scanned it hurriedly.

"Miss Lawson," he read aloud, mechanically.

Also scribbled hastily on the side:

"Come as quickly as you can."

"If it is an automobile she is in," Webster suggested, "perhaps Mr. Elliston's company would not be disagreeable. You could put him in front and let him talk to the chauffeur. I believe Dr. Lawson's driver is a negro, is he not?"

"Not a bad idea at all," Keough explained. "Come, Mr. Elliston, off to Darktown!"

CHAPTER IX

The Problem from a Tonneau

"What I can quite understand," Mr. Elliston said, as they drove off, "is the feeling of personal repugnance you have for the negro, and the negro for you also; but I don't see why that should affect your politics."

"Nor why the races should be separated on the street cars, railways, churches, elevators, etc. That is what you are going to say, isn't it?" Miss Lawson questioned.

"Only partly," Elliston continued. "I wanted your view point badly enough to come a thousand miles for it. I want to know where the line stops, so I am going to ask you a very pointed question. If a nice black fellow, with plenty of education, refinement, etc. — "

"And money," Keough put in.

"Well, I say if such a fellow were to fall in love with one of the ordinary white working girls — "

"O, put it the other way!" Miss Lawson suggested. "If a white man of ordinary, etc."

"Well, that will do then," Elliston continued. "Suppose there were a girl — practically white — with the 'one drop,' as you call it, in her veins; and suppose she were perfectly honest, virtuous, well educated, and in every way a lady, and a young white man were to fall in love with her without knowing of her 'drop,' and later found it out — he being a Southerner—now what would he do? What would he do, Miss Lawson?"

"Really," she answered, while her heart beat violently, "Mr. Keough should answer you."

The question—at last—how she had longed to put it to him! She trembled now, lest some mischance should prevent his answering it—and lest he should answer it.

The question?

"What do you think, Mr. Keough?"

"Well," Roy replied, slowly, "it is very hard to say. I should think, however, that if he had grown tired of her at all, he would leave her and sink himself in a new country; if he loved her, he would probably make his peace with God and blow his brains out."

The woman looked mistily to the right, and the New York journalist drew out his notebook.

"*View point the same as that of nice Northern people,*" he wrote.

"Mr. Webster told me of a beautiful picture a lady graduate of his school painted," Elliston continued. "I believe it is called 'THE END.' I guess you know its *motif?* What's become of the girl? Really, I'd like to meet her."

"To see her?" Miss Lawson suggested. "Really, Mr. Elliston—you will not think me rude—all such are without the pale in the South; they belong to the world we never mention."

It was neatly done, Roy thought.

Luckily, they were already on the outskirts of Darktown.

"It is only fair to say," Miss Lawson suggested, "that this is not the Fifth Avenue of the colored section."

"Right," Keough added. "There are parts of Atlanta where the best negroes lives. There are neat homes, and their inmates are ladies and gentlemen. But look at this!"

Squalid misery—ill-odored poverty—dirt—filth—full cabins—an air stench-laden, reeking with disease—crowded with the negro poor, whose black brood played ill clad—half naked in the doorways, overflowed into the streets and filled them with more filth, more disease, more stench.

"Say, let's take a little spin in the country before it gets too dark," Elliston suggested.

Keough smiled.

"What are you interested in them for, anyway?" Miss Lawson asked. "Do you think they are people?"

"Unfairly put, Miss Lawson," Roy laughed.

"Why, yes," Elliston answered, "I think they are people, a distinct people, and—"

"What of them?" she asked, when he paused. "What is their future? Are you arguing for amalgamation in your articles?"

"So far as I know," Elliston replied, with curious sadness, "the yellowest of our abominable yellow journals would not stand for such a series of articles as that. *There is a wonderful store of mischievous misinformation about the North even in Atlanta,*" he continued. "Webster was talking about the Third Race. Northern men don't want one, and are not afraid that there will ever be one. We've no idea of marrying negroes, despite the hysterics of your melo-dramatic novels, nor of marrying Turks nor Chinese; *and we do not expect our Southern friends to do so.* We don't see many negroes, and those that we do see are as decent as very many of the European immigrants who swarm in on us every year. We have a hydra-headed race problem of our own, very different from yours in the South. Some of the aspects of the latter are so unfamiliar to me as hardly to seem real. We *can't* feel about them as you do!"

"A hundred years ago," she continued, "one-seventh of the globe was white; to-day, one-half; to-morrow — what is the use of fooling with them at all? Down South here we see their numbers constantly decreasing in comparison with us."

"Decreasing? Why, I thought they were taking the country!" Elliston exclaimed.

"One white man," she replied, "has accumulated more wealth since the war than the whole race of ten million of them. And as for numbers, did you know South Carolina's negro population increased only one-fourth as much, proportionately, during the last decade as Pennsylvania's or Massachusetts'? I believe Tennessee's didn't increase at all, did it, Mr. Keough?"

"She is pretty nearly correct, Mr. Elliston. Philadelphia, Washington, and Baltimore are the largest negro cities of the hemisphere. But here we are at the *Commonwealth* Building. I shall look out for your articles, Mr. Elliston."

The New York journalist vanished toward the elevator.

"It is really a pity to stop now, Mr. Keough," Miss Lawson suggested. "See, the moonlight has just come. Do you not love the moonlight enough for a spin to the country?"

He thought of his unfinished "Song and Story." It would be the first time he had left it for any man or woman.

"If you go, I go with you," he answered.

He entered the car then, and the driver started out Peachtree at a merry clip.

"To Oakdale, Will," she whispered, standing to adjust her wraps, "for the 9:30 train."

Then to Keough —

"How far would you go with me?" she ventured.

He turned and looked. Her eyes were full upon him, and the lights showed a compelling loveliness in her face. She was leaning forward as if his answer meant something to her.

He took her hand gently in his, and whispered:

"To the end of the King's Highway!"

"Ah, glorious cup!" she murmured, so low that he heard nothing. "I will drink of thee to-night — drink deep of thee — if I die to-morrow!"

CHAPTER X

The Pack Forms

The black man paused upon the threshold. Should he really go in, after all? His anger still burned within him, and the fierce-flamed love for the Third-Race woman. To learn of her whereabouts, to force this ignoble father of hers to divulge them—that was the only course left him. By every right of priority she belonged to him. What though the *Commonwealth* reporter had carried her away? It was a deathly deception. She was pardonable. Who could resist an invitation into the glow of the White Circle? But the white man would not pardon her. He would bellow with rage and drive her forth to find a mate among the black people. What a mad, mad course she was on! How awful her doom when discovered! Perhaps too, the white man knew, and only wanted another mistress. God! how his heart throbbed! There was no longer any hesitation in his steps. He opened the door abruptly.

"Do you want to see the maid?" a waiting patient asked.

"No, madam; I have come to see Dr. Lawson. If the maid is near—here is my card."

The negro girl had seen the newcomer.

"These are Dr. Lawson's office hours," she said, as softly as possible. "You know he confines his practice entirely to whites. You might see him for a moment when he goes to lunch, or call at his back door to-night."

"I will see him now. Kindly say to him that a man who will not be put off waits for him at the door."

The negro woman stood back amazed.

"He is stark mad!" she ejaculated, and shut the door in his face.

Kongo waited for a moment—long enough for her to have returned, long enough for Dr. Lawson to have excused himself from his patient—and then stepped boldly into the elegant waiting room of Atlanta's greatest dentist.

"I have come to see Dr. Lawson," he commenced, in a steady voice, to the maid, "and I *will* see him."

There was something about his look, some reminder of the avenger who came forth from his wrong to kill, that made a timid woman patient by the window shriek aloud.

In a moment Dr. Lawson stood smiling in the doorway between his operating room and his parlors.

"I want to see you a moment, Dr. Lawson," Copelin said, calmly. "We have business together of a sort that may not be put off."

It took the dentist a moment to understand.

"Are you the cause of all this commotion?" he then asked.

"No," Kongo replied; "you are. But I should rather finish what I have to say in private."

"What is your name, man, and what do you mean?" he asked, seeing no point to it all.

The fierce flames of a life's passion vibrated in the voice of the negro professor as he replied:

"My name is Kongo Copelin. I love *your daughter.* I have come to ask you where she is. I have a right to ask it," he continued, while the dazed dentist gazed on him in amazement. "She is my promised wife, even if she has run away with Roy Keough."

Then he understood.

The light began to glow in his eyes, his muscles twitched, his teeth set, his hands clinched, his jaws gripped one another, knowing well it was too late for words. The negro professor had come unarmed, save by a righteous cause; and when he saw death glaring at him, reached back for his penknife. The dentist fairly trembled with rage. He did not see the negro reach back for his knife. His whole powerful body prepared itself in ligament, bone, and muscle for the spring of a wild animal that hated and would kill!

The two men clashed. The dentist fell heavily to the floor. A red stream spurted from his breast.

A half dozen lady patients shrieked as he fell. The negro maid trembled as she thought of its awful meaning, as she heard the white pack at the heels of the "negro wild beast."

Then Copelin rose from the floor, only half understanding what he had done. He had not meant to do this thing— only to avenge publicly the shame of a woman of his people. He saw the red pool on the floor and the white face beneath him. His instincts, the instincts of the black folk who had striven and slain in the jungle for untold generations, took hold of him.

With a wild moan of terror, he fled.

Out into the streets first he ran, guided by the ancient instincts, on toward the busy triangle before Silverman's

Corner—on—on—with one word upon his lips—
Decatur Street!

A white man saw him and called:

"Stop, thief!"

The woman who had screamed called down from the window:

"He's a murderer! Arrest him quick! He has killed Dr. Lawson!"

The negro maid looked out and measured the distance with her eye.

"He's running for one of the dives," she said. "He's got a good lead; he may make it. God have mercy on us all!"

Then the white pack began to form. A policeman took the runner and his errand in at a glance.

"Stop him! Head him off! He's making for the dives!" he called.

But Kongo had heard, he, the son of jungle men—the dim memories of a thousand ancestors who had fled from the pack drove him on—on—

Another policeman fired, but put up his pistol as he saw the crowded streets. The shot brought a score of men who followed the runner in close pursuit.

But the man ran unencumbered by numbers—single—he knew where—ran as a man would run for his life, with the yelping of the pack at his heels.

In a moment he had reached Decatur Street, in another he had sprung into a barroom door, in a few more he was out at the back door and into another—among his fellows, scores of them, who understood.

A glance told the story. He was hid safely away in a jiffy.

The pack yelped at the dive their quarry had entered,

battered down the door, then fairly bellowed with baffled anger as they found he was not there.

But another negro man suddenly sprang, seemingly terrified, from a side room and fled down the street.

The pack followed; a policeman fired and missed. The negro fairly flew down Decatur Street.

The jungle men who had hid Copelin away looked after him and muttered:

"It's Jackson; he saved Will Johnson twice. He's a good 'un!"

Then, when the pack had almost despaired of the pursuit, the quarry suddenly stumbled and fell. In a moment they were on him. A policeman grabbed him by the collar.

"Don't touch him, boys! The law'll get him quick enough. He's as good as a dead 'un now!"

So they bore him back in triumph to the jail.

The captured jungle man said no word.

"By George, boys," cried one of the best runners among the pursuers, "we were lucky to get him. Forty saloons on Decatur Street! Twenty-five hundred nigger loafers in them! Who'd 'a' thought it?"

Then he gave Jackson a cuff.

"You d——n black beast!" he said. "You didn't get to hide this time!"

CHAPTER XI

The Lair

When the noise and the tumult were over and the dust had settled again in the highway, the door behind which Kongo Copelin had hid was opened softly, and the prisoner was told that he might now come out with safety.

"Have they gone already?" he queried.

"Yeah; we got 'em fooled. Say, what'd you do?"

But Kongo was too surprised to notice the question.

"Why, I have been momentarily expecting them to break down the door. What did you do to get them away?"

"Same old thing—swapped horses an' got 'em on 'nother man's trail. Ed Jackson saved yer. They got him in the 'Black Maria' now. Say, you're an eddicated nigger, ain't yer? What in the h——l you doin' down here with us?"

"I had a fight with a white man," Copelin replied, "and I killed him. I could think of nowhere else to come. Can you hide me for a while?"

"That's sho' our job," the "proprietor" assured him. "We hid Bill Ammons long enough. He's got twelve white women already. Wus'n Will Johnson, ain't he?"

Copelin shuddered. This was a stratum of his race of which he, though a negro, knew nothing. They were the jungle men, the wild beasts who could not be tamed. Like their legendary ancestors, they had gone back into the forest and turned again into gorilla-men. He looked upon the "proprietor," with his padded lips; his filthy, kinky head; his stealthy, animal tread; and noted the wild look of the untamable in his coal-black eyes and the distended nostrils which long centuries had fashioned so that by odor his life might be saved whose wit had failed.

"I done a few stunts myse'f," the "proprietor" continued. "I killed a white man in South C'liny. Slid out for Alabam; got a white woman out there. Come back to Atlanta. This town's the best 'un to hide in I ever saw. Niggers sticks together, and don't peach none on nobody. There's old Garrabrant out there at the bar. If these d——n white p'licemen knowed he was down here, they'd burn up Decatur Street. Pardner, you look kinder sheety. Come on an' have a drink."

To this, then, he—Kongo Copelin—had descended. To these jungle men he was indebted for his life. They had counted him as a brother, and so instinctively protected him. Yet he loathed them and all their kind.

The "proprietor" led him out to the bar. For a moment it seemed to him that he was in the jungle again. A forest of black, animal faces gazed at him, some with drunken leers.

"Sporty nigger," one remarked. "What'd he do?"

"Killed a white man, the 'prop.' says."

"Nearly got him, didn't they?"

"Sho' did. He's the fourth come in this week."

"Goin' ter be trouble, too. Too many of 'em comin'. Seen the *Press* to-day? Look a-here!"

The speaker drew out a copy of the *Evening Press*, whose

extra was being cried on the street, and read from the editorial columns:

"No law of God or man can hold back the vengeance of our white men upon such a criminal. If necessary, we will double and treble and quadruple the law of Moses and hang off-hand the criminal; or, failing to find that a remedy, we will hang two, three, or four of the negroes nearest to the crime, until it is no longer feared in all this Southern land that we inhabit and love."

"Good God! Dey ain't talkin' dat way 'bout killin' a white man, is dey?"

"Naw! Will Johnson's got another white woman!"

"How many nigger women has these d——n po' white trash got? Where'd he go?"

"Down the street, then back here. He's in the 'prop.'s' room."

Copelin heard their words and shuddered. He was a negro, but not such a one as these. He was a negro man—a gentleman, as were most of his race.

But they were types of the NEGRO WILD BEAST.

And he had been saved by fleeing to their lair.

For very exhaustion's sake he drank the whisky the "prop." gave him, and looked about him. "Black-faced animals"—he could call them nothing else—crowded around the bar, mingling snatches of old plantation songs, remnants of better days, with curses and filthy jokes. He finally sat down almost unnoticed in a chair to think. Then he noticed a curious thing. Whether they stood or sat, these chronic criminals turned their eyes steadily in one direction, and it was not toward the door.

"Here's to her health!" he heard a drunken vagrant shout.

At that he saw the great majority look upward at a picture on the wall. He followed their gaze.

He saw THE QUEEN OF THE LAIR.

It was a large chromo, suggestively colored, showing a nude white woman lying under a tree upon the leaves of the forest. Around and on the other sides — in fact, everywhere about the walls — there were other smaller pictures of similar suggestiveness; but this one was so gorgeously colored, so lifelike in size and seeming, that these jungle men looked at it and feasted their eyes upon it. To them it was all. It was sometimes called "Social Equality," sometimes "Criminal Assault," sometimes by other names; but these animals of the forest saw names and distinctions but dimly. They only knew that whisky fired the passions of hell within them, and "The Queen of the Lair" gave visions of heaven.

Copelin looked at the picture and then at the passion-lit eyes of these outcast men, and forgot that he was a man-slayer.

"Great merciful Jesus!" he exclaimed. "And these are my people! Why do not white men see — *why can't they know where and how the peaceful, unoffending negro man is turned into the passion-driven beast of the jungle?*"

Then he remembered the words of the Third-Race girl, the beautiful woman whom he had accounted his:

"What would you do? If not one-tenth part of your blood were negro, and that not of an ignoble strain; if, when dissociated from negroes, men counted you white; if your training and ambitions and education all identified you with the White Circle, would you want to be called 'nigger?' Would you allow your life to be forced back with the jungle people?"

She had said that, and he had not till now understood.

But as he looked around him at the sodden ignorance, the reeking filth, the blatant crime, the bestial animality, he understood.

He had seen the NEGRO WILD BEAST.

All the while that he studied their faces there was in his mind a subdued consciousness as of the falling of a mighty cataract or the roaring of a wind through the forest. Little by little he came to hear it. When at last the full noise burst upon his ear, he noticed a considerable diminution in the sea of black faces that had thronged the dive. Also the "proprietor" was hastening nervously here and there, muttering something to himself.

"Too many of 'em at last! D——n such luck!" Copelin heard.

"It's a raid, sho's gun's iron!" a watcher shouted from the street.

"Better git into your closet or hide out there, you—you eddicated nigger!" the "prop." called.

"De whole d——n po-lees is a-comin'!" yelled the man from the street. "I'se gwine to shine my greasy!"

A moment later rock smashed through the window and shivered half a dozen bottles on the bar.

"It's a d——n sight wuss'n a raid," the "prop." muttered; "*it's a mob!*"

CHAPTER XII

The Riot

For centuries the unclean rivers pour their mud and silt into the bosom of the fair-faced sea. Slowly does their burden accumulate along the coast line. All the while the pressure grows more tense, and the heat lines of the inner earth rise toward the surface. Then there comes a day, fair, perhaps, and unoffending, as that eventful day of September came to Atlanta, when the tension becomes too great, the subsurface heat too fierce, and a fearful collapse follows. The volcano belches, the calm surface of things becomes a pandemonium of terror, the fountains of the unknown deep are broken up, and over all there broods a horror of great darkness. But from it, and eventually towering over it all, there rises the eternal mountain peak linked hand in hand with his brothers.

It was so with Atlanta on September 22, 1906. Years before there had been a day in her history when the order she loved and founded had passed into a new order; and that she might remember it, Sherman baptized her with fire. While the ancient order lasted—let this be said to those who curse it—her women were safe and her daughters knew no fear. With a singular lack of foresight and a carelessness which, unexcused by ignorance, was criminal, the men who founded the republic of which she was a part had sent into the African jungle and hunted down the savages there, to fetch them for labor in the New World. The ineffaceable sadness of the hunted thing, line bred for a thousand generations, was in their eyes. They blinked at the light of the White Circle at first, and wondered why they must now be taught new games to play at. Guarded and controlled, they learned to do the heavy work of the South, until the chisels and saws and hammers and hoes were all held by black hands, from the Potomac to the Rio Grande. They were dressed like men and taught to do work like them, and at last they became men; and after a while along came the good doctrine of the universal brotherhood of man, its coat tails tightly gripped by manhood suffrage. Followed liberty. Thereafter most still reached out their hands and clung to white men. Some few went back into the jungle.

From the shadows of their forest night these last came forth as passion drove, and ever with increasing frequency. The white South saw it and brushed away the tormenting prophet, saying: "It will be all right!" The black gentlemen of the South saw it, and cried: "God save us!" Atlanta saw it, and knew it would be her part who led the race to suffer first.

For months before the explosion came the nervous tension of the city had steadily augmented. There had been story after story of how the beast had come forth from his lair and glutted his passion upon white women. All this was in the papers. But the unnamable terror of the black women was not, though they, too, suffered. Men had turned sick at reading the details, knowing the unmentionable things that were never printed. A school-teacher, perhaps, passing in the evening on her way home from a country school, waylaid and assaulted! A man murdered at night as he lay in his bed, and unspeakable horrors perpetrated upon his wife and daughter! These things Atlanta saw, while her blood boiled within her.

Steadily they grew more frequent, and were accompanied with greater boldness and horrors, until the beast feared not to attack his victims in the city itself. Woman after woman, girl after girl, child after child, the jungle men assaulted; and even the babes were not exempt.

At last it could be stood no longer. Another straw and the back was broken.

Then came a deed of horror. A man of Yankee descent had brought his young wife South and built her a little home at the edge of a pine grove near the city. One morning a jungle man came to the home, prying about it as a wild beast would look at the house its quarry had built. The man spoke to him, and the negro asked some silly question in response. The woman and her husband were worried; for though they had lived only four years in the South, the horror of the great darkness had fallen near enough to them for all to know its terrors. Yet the man must needs go away to his work, for only by his labor could they get along in the world. The nearest neighbor was to keep an eye open for the beast. The man went. Returning, he found scores of white men in his yard. He knew that the jungle man had come and gone on his passion-driven errand. He had fled, and the woman could give no accurate description of him.

Those who gathered there before that little green cottage knew then that the storm had gathered.

So when the next morning had come, and no word of the capture of the negro wild beast with it, men left pistols in the hands of their wives at home; and the telephones kept ringing, lest all might not be well. The normal gayety of the city was gone, and an ominous quiet had come in its stead. Those who talked little were silent altogether, and the garrulous spoke almost in whispers. The police force was to be doubled on October 1; this was only September 22. Perhaps even that would avail but little.

And pitiful was the terror by day and night of the sober mass of law-abiding black people—afraid of the rapists of their own race and the rioters of the other.

Saturday afternoon came and found the eternal crowd before Silverman's Corner swelled by hundreds of farmers and country folk who had come to town for the week-end shopping. Also, it was still summer in Atlanta, and the half holiday had poured out its thousands into the streets.

In the early afternoon there came the first terror cry, and, to those who had heard it in fear before, it was like the hacking cough of a little babe at night to an anxious mother—a cough that no medicine could stop.

"Another assault!"

The newsboys took up the cry, and handed the extra out to the trembling hands.

"Paper, mister? Paper? All about another assault!"

The papers were quickly scattered and read, and a "hillbilly," with a little mustache growing on the end of his red nose, but whose wife was alone in their little home in the piny woods ten miles away, muttered to himself:

"D——n 'em! They're a lot of hell-lit beasts!"

His neighbor heard and volubly approved.

"We are goin' to have to exterminate 'em yet," he said.

"Why in the h——l don't you drive 'em into the Gulf

of Mexico?" an Ohio employee of one of the big insurance companies, whose office building towered above the speakers, questioned, hotly. "We burn 'em out up in our country."

"What in the h——l would we do fer hands on the farm?" the "hillbilly" replied. "But, by G——d, it's comin' to that, and I'm ready to start it!"

"Why do you not catch them and let the law take its course?" a handsome, well-groomed journalist from New York asked.

"Ketch 'em! My God, man, you might as well talk o' ketchin' a mite on a settin' hen! D——n 'em, that's what we got ag'in' 'em!" the "hillbilly" yelled. "*They hide their criminals!*"

Mr. Elliston drew out his notebook. There was a point for the *Modern Trend.*

"What I hate about 'em is," the Ohio man continued, "they ain't people. I'll be—"

He stopped there, for they heard a different noise—a low, moaning sound as of distant winds muttering in the pines. Then above it came a sharp, shrill cry.

"*Second assault to-day!* Extra, mister? Here's your *Evening Press!* All about the second assault!"

The "hillbilly" clinched his fists and ran forward to buy his paper.

By this time the crowd had grown till, upon the great triangle at the intersection of Decatur and Peachtree Streets, over a thousand men had collected. A premonition of impending evil overshadowed them. There was a singular quiet on all sides, as if the nervous tension were great. As the darkness began to fall, fathers hastily closed up their offices and hurried homeward to their wives.

Anxious women looked out of the windows of thousands of homes that night waiting for their protectors to come. With never so much joy before did the girls of Atlanta rush into the arms of their fathers. The shadow of unnamable fear was upon every home.

So the streets were left for boys and "hillbillies" and red necks, with here and there a responsible man.

CHAPTER XIII

Jungle Justice

"Where's the police?" the countryman with the little red mustache on the end of his nose asked of a young hoodlum who stood by him.

"Raidin' the dives down on Decatur Street."

"Listen to that!"

Again the cry:

"*Third assault!* Paper, mister?"

"By G——d, there's goin' to be trouble here, and right now, at that! Come on, boys, let's give 'em h——l!"

"I just heard two little white boys was held up and robbed in the suburbs," the hoodlum answered.

"And look a-yonder!" a gamin cried. "Did you see that nigger grab that white woman's pocketbook?"

"Gee-muny-chrismus! They're fightin'!" he yelled, as a white man sprang on the negro and bore him down.

Two other negroes came instantly to the aid of the first, and a rough-and-tumble fight ensued. At last the crowd became noisy, the tension began to give way, the lightning flashed, and the storm broke.

And above the tumult could be heard the shrill cry of the newsboy:

"*Fourth assault!* Here's the *Evening Press!* All about the fourth assault!"

Then the mob formed. To the first two thousand was

77

quickly added a third, a fourth, a fifth, a sixth, a seventh. The night had come, and the saloons poured out their drunken revelers. For some it was a game; for most it was the long-delayed revenge against the beast from whom they had suffered. The mob was, for the most part, formed of the under class—the whites who came in most intimate contact with the jungle men. Added to these were the irresponsibles—the youth, the drunken, the hoodlums. But here and there among them, and ever the moving spirits, were men whose wives were alone in cottages on the by-streets or at the edge of distant piny woods. And the burden of their cry was:

"D——n 'em! *They hide their criminals*! They run to the dens, they flee to their lairs, and are lost in a sea of jungle faces!"

Farther back in the distant centuries (and not so far but that it may be known to be) there was the forest where the white man dwelt as half man, half beast, of whom to this present hour there are none so tame, so cultured and locked up, but will have a wild trick of his ancestors. To these all who thronged the streets of the great city that night the mob demon came. He kindled hate in their breasts and murder in their hearts. He made them forget the difference between negro men and negro wild beasts, between those who stood willingly as near the White Circle as they might and those who chose the night life of the jungle. To maim, to bruise, to curse, to kill! This they hastened to do.

Yet in their minds there was a jungle justice. These black people—did they choose to stand together, to hide their woman slayers? Then let the punishment be measured out to all. There was enough to go around to the whole race. They sheltered the wild beasts in their dives and dens; they were participants in the crime. If they would sin as a race, let them so suffer. That was the rude forest philosophy of the first white mob in the South who went out to murder the jungle men.

What so terrible as the blue eye of the Anglo-Saxon when it is fairly red with anger, no matter whether that eye rests in a reeling head or in the sockets of hoodlums? The black man found it so that night. The unreasoning hate of it was atavistic. A barber shaving a white man shot down, and a bootblack busy at an Aryan's foot; a negro woman dragged from a street car and thrown through a shop window with a crash; Pullman porters mobbed from their near-by cars — these were but incidents that marked the rising, unreasoning fury of the rioters.

And still the shrill cry of the newsboys:

"Fourth assault!"

The "hillbilly," whose wife was alone in the little cottage by the edge of the piny woods, heard it.

"Come on, boys, let's burn 'em out!" he cried.

Already the mob was as well armed as the hardware stores of the city could arm them. Now they broke into others, and added the pawnshops and dens and dives of Decatur Street to give the firearms wherewith to hunt down the black man as well as black beast.

Then the awful storm burst. No longer was there any discrimination at all. Beating, killing, wounding, cursing — the mob went wild. Even the fire hose could scarce dampen more than the outskirts of it. The police were far away down on Decatur Street. The military could not be called out.

The passion of the rioters grew, the blood lust increased.

They overflowed into the near-by streets, hunting for the black man, eager for murder, craving their blood.

Then the strange thing happened. Into the notorious old train shed rolled the midnight train from Dunvegan. From it an aged man stepped lightly, thinking of the sermon he was to preach in the great Eastminster Church on the morrow. Pleasant were his memories of this eager city, upon all of whose children the Eternal Urge was placed — of the magnificent church which had once called him to its pastorate. Of these things he was thinking when the noise of the unfettered storm smote upon his ear.

For a moment he was bewildered.

Then at his feet a negro fell.

"O God!" the man yelled, with the fright of the last hour in his words. "Save me, boss, save me! They're killin' the niggers! Save me, for God's sake! Save me, save me!"

His voice rose like the shriek of a soul in hell whose God was passing him by.

On his heels followed the mob.

"Kill him! D——n him, kill him! *He shelters the criminals of his race!* Shoot him!"

In a moment the aged man from Dunvegan was the center of the howling, bloodthirsty mob. The negro, already bloody with beating, crouched imploringly at his feet.

Then the Dunvegan minister cast his light cloak upon the kneeling black man and whispered to him:

"Hold yourself steady; I must stand on your back to speak to these people. There! On your hands and knees. Steady now — "

"He stepped upon the broad back of the negro man and beckoned for silence."

Then he stepped upon the broad back of the negro man and beckoned for silence.

The mob wavered. Perhaps it was some one who would make announcement of another assault—perhaps some news of importance. Then, too, he was a gentleman of distinguished mien, and stood unflinchingly before them upon the black platform he had made.

Then some one who had heard and seen him before in the great Eastminster Church shouted:

"Hush! It's Dr. Wilfong!"

CHAPTER XIV

THE SPIRIT OF THE OLD SOUTH

He spoke distinctly and with commanding clearness, kindly, as if he understood. They had not listened long before they knew that it was the voice of their master that night. The calm look of the man, the face that knew no fear, the spirit of infinite command about him.

Arthur Elliston stood in the mob, notebook in hand, listening.

"Who is he?" some one asked him.

"He is the *Old South* come to life again!" Elliston replied. "Hush, and you will hear something worth listening to."

The old gentleman spoke from the negro's back. He also loved Atlanta, even the careless boyishness of the city. Perhaps that superabundant exuberance carried them sometimes too far and their enthusiasm was misdirected. With a smile that for seventy years had won men's confidence, he told them that he was standing on the back of a negro man, just as white men in the South had been doing since the first Dutch ship brought the black folk to the New World. They were big and strong and brawny, yet they were a child race, and no Southern man with the ancient chivalry of his fathers in his blood would fail to protect the innocent among them. (Here there was a murmur as of approval that ran through the crowd.)

"In my younger days," he continued, "when I went as pastor to the manse in the little village from which I came to-night, I found there an old negro man who for many years had been the 'boy' for my predecessor in the church. Some days later, in arranging the yards, I had occasion to plant some flowers, and asked the elderly negro to dig up a violet bed which seemed to me to have been planted in the wrong place. The gray-haired darky looked at me a little strangely, and said: 'Yes, sir, boss.' A week later I noticed that the violet bed was still there, and spoke to him again, this time rather sharply. Again the ancient darky said: 'Yes, sir, boss.' But when another week passed and the violets were not removed, then I called the old man to me and told him that if he was to continue in my service, his first lesson was to be that of obedience, and asked him why he had failed twice to do my bidding. The old darky's eyes filled up at that, and he said: 'Boss, when me an' my marster was little boys, befo' dey done buy dis ole house from him fer to be de manse, we planted dem violets dere; an', boss, I jes' done been tryin', but I can't, boss — I can't dig dem violets up what we planted when we was boys.' Then I laid my hands upon the old darky's shoulder and blessed him. If you look closely, you will see three violets in my buttonhole; they came from that old man's violet bed. And, men — I speak to you as Southrons — who will dig up the beds of friendship our fathers and theirs planted in the times before the war?"

The pastor of Dunvegan paused there and looked about him. Men were turning here and there in the multitude and taking away their fellows with them. Little by little the mob began to disperse, one or two looking mistily at their neighbors.

Arthur Elliston stood still, watching the crowds. To him it was all more or less a revelation. He had heard of the part played by such ministers as Dr. Wilfong in the South; but it did not seem possible that a preacher could really lead still in such affairs, much less at such moments as this. Here, then, in this handsome old man from the village church was a power to be reckoned with. That was the way he made note of it for the readers of the *Modern Trend.* As he was writing it down, the Ohio man came up.

"Say, that was a swell talk he gave them, wasn't it?" he commented.

"It was, indeed. He's just about quelled this end of the riot."

"Gee, but it was great sport running those niggers!" a new voice put in. "Sorry the old man came along. A fellow from N'York and myself chased one over the country, through cotton patches, brier thickets, and I don't know what else."

"Where are you from?" the journalist queried.

"Travel out of Boston—born in Worcester. We shot at him more than a dozen times, but he got away. What's that the old man's saying to the nigger?"

Dr. Wilfong had stepped down from his improvised platform and taken his wrap from off the back of the black man who had fled to him for protection. The negro had risen, and stood upon his feet, half fearfully, half trustfully.

"You had a very narrow escape, my man. A little more and they would have gotten you. I think you are safe now; but perhaps you had best go along with me. I am to stop at Dr. Lawson's home to-night. You might guide me there, for I have missed the carriage in this mob. The Doctor, I am sure, will let you stay with his servants to-night."

The negro turned ashy pale.

"My kind sir," he said, "I will guide you there, but I—I cannot—stay."

"It doesn't matter. Come, let us hurry. I understand the Doctor has not quite recovered from an accident that befell him last week. Come, we must be going."

But the negro stood stock still, trembling from head to foot.

"Isn't—he—dead?" he almost shouted.

"Dead? Why, no, he isn't dead. Dead men do not send telegrams as he has done to me this day. He was—"

"O, dear God!" the negro cried. "Then I am not a murderer! I shall not be a jungle man!"

"Your name, fellow?" the Doctor asked, for by now they were alone on the corner. "And why do you act so strangely?"

"Sir, my name is 'Kongo Copelin,'" he replied; "and I am the man who stabbed Dr. Lawson."

As he spoke, Dr. Wilfong felt a light touch on his arm, and turned to see a well-groomed white man standing beside him.

"This is Dr. Wilfong?" the stranger asked. "Elliston is my name. I am one of the editors of the *Modern Trend*. I should like very much to see you for a moment to-morrow, Doctor, if you can find the time."

"I am entirely at your service, sir, on the day after to-morrow. Dr. Lawson is my host—"

"Then I shall avail myself of the opportunity Monday morning. I want to glean from you the attitude of the *Best South on the negro problem*."

"The Best South, the negro problem," the distinguished old man mused, sadly. "Ah, sir, what is the negro problem? *Rakes and rum*—white rakes, white men's rum. Some talk of the danger of 'amalgamation,' as if there were a mulatto in the South whose father was not a white man. *This is the negro problem*—white lepers that father the Third Race, and white liquor that fathers the black rapist; *and for which of these are the kindly black folk responsible?* But I shall give it all to you Monday," he added, with a smile. "To-morrow I give to God."

CHAPTER XV

The King's Highway

Miss Lawson seemed unusually quiet, as if in trouble, while the motor car sped on; but then, unhaloed by sadness, what face is perfectly beautiful?

"What an odd man that was!" she began. "Why is he so interested in—in them?" pointing toward the driver ahead.

"He is an editor," Keough suggested, amused, "and they must have their 'problems.'"

"I have read about 'the problem' till I am bewildered by it. Yet do you know I sometimes wonder, despite what I said to him a moment ago—I wonder how any one can doubt what will be the final outcome of it."

"The outcome?"

"I was reading a book only last night. I remember rather indistinctly the prophecy of the last chapter. 'About the two hundredth century of our era,' it said, 'there will be only one race on earth—rather small in stature, light colored, in which anthropologists might perhaps be able to discern indications of English and Chinese descent.'"

"That," he said, "we will never permit!"

For a moment she was silent, while the shadow of terror swept swiftly over her face.

"Ah," she at length replied, "what have *we* to do with that which is permitted? We should consult our gods and our ancient monuments. There were Romans once who despised their slaves—now the Italian. There were Normans once who despised the Engles—now the Englishmen. There were Teutons once who despised the negro—now the eternal now—there are, there will be—"

She paused, gazing at him wistfully.

"There will be?" he asked.

"The American?" she inquired, in turn.

He seemed busy with his thoughts.

"Silently—ah, so silently!—and unnoticed," she continued, softly, "the human race drives forward to its destiny, like the great family of the solar system speeding many miles per second toward its goal of mystery in the constellation Hercules."

" 'To wash a black,' Geil says, 'is to lose one's soap,'" he suggested, grimly. "But what shall we say of washing the immoral white rakes who betray black and white and God by their shameless seduction of the black women? To cleanse him is to change the leopard's spots."

"Perhaps. But where now are the Aryans who left the common home of their race and passed the Hindu-Kush to conquer the fertile plains of India? Their children are black to-day. They did the thing no race can do and live—they left their isothermal line. It was fifty mean in his Aryan home; it was seventy in his new home. The subtropics sapped his vitality, and he was himself overcome by the negroid's climate. Only his religion and his caste are left. We whites are now almost in the subtropics. See what such a climate did to the fair-haired Aryans who chose Greece and Italy as their home!"

"And there were the Persians, too," he assented. "The hot plain of the Euphrates did the same for them, but—"

"There was ancient Hellas," she interrupted—"Hellas, filled with decadent whites in a climatically foreign land. The Dorian came, revivifying the race. Then the age of Pericles; then more decadence. Then Greece, over which the world weeps pityingly, remembering her former honors. Did not Solomon say: 'The thing which hath been is the thing which shall be?' Men may learn to turn back the flood in its madness, to train the storm for service; but the inexorable law of climate and race—who can change it, save he who can command God as his servant? And then, also, who can tell what the negro's possibilities are? He is a young race—yet."

Roy Keough listened. All this he had thought out long ago.

"But there is a thing," he answered, "about which I would not speak, except to one who could understand that my motive is not sinister. You have no right to speak of the negroid as a young race. It is of them all the oldest, the first to flourish and—to grow old. It built the first Babylon. It preceded the Semite in the valley of the Euphrates, and by the Ganges grew as great as it could before the Aryan came down from the hills of the Hindu-Kush. It is the oldest of all the races—first in birth and first in death. There was a Mesozoic Age—you learned of it in college—with its reptiles, hideous, monstrous, tremendously powerful. There also was an age of ferns and an age of fishes. Each has passed, as has passed the age of the black race, the first age—not of iron, silver, or gold, but of wood. In it they flowered in a sort of crude, grotesque civilization till, senescent, the Semite came and took away their place by the Nile and the Euphrates, and the Brahmanic Aryan made of them hewers of wood and drawers of water."

"But you forget," she interrupted, "that one may absorb what one may not create. The Japs used the German cannon to the best purpose. They say: 'Look at the civilization around you; make it yours, follow its logic. It will give youth to the oldest of races.'"

"If it were only a possible thing! God knows I have prayed for it, white man though I am! But each animal has its covering—the bird, feathers; the fish, scales; the cat, fur; the dog, hair. Each race has its civilization, its life. Any adoption of it by a widely variant people must be only temporary. There was the American Indian, the Maori, the Hawaiian. To these the Aryan's civilization was poison. They may smear themselves over with white paint, but they will never think the world in Aryan categories. Therein lies their infinite hopelessness. They are an old folk and a kindly folk—and a trustful. Their thoughts have form and color which may not be changed. They have come down through the ages to the twentieth century. So has the kangaroo. The Maori and the Dodo—they are types. There were Romans—once; there were Phenicians—once. The mammoth *was*. So some day they shall say of the negro: 'He was!'"

"It was thus with the tree fern, the mastodon, the cave bear," she murmured.

"But, Laura, dear, what unearthly affair could have put these things, these needless worries, in your mind?" he asked.

It was now time.

A suspicious moisture came into her eyes, the while she muttered to herself: "I despise to do it this way, but there is no other!"

She leaned forward toward him:

"O, if I could only tell you something!" she murmured, slowly.

Not for a moment did those wonderful, dark eyes cease from their absorbed gaze into his. A deep flush was creeping swiftly into her cheeks. He could see that her breath was coming quickly, and her lips quivered, as if they could scarcely conquer their feelings.

He caught her hand under the lap robe.

"Laura, you are in trouble!" he exclaimed, softly, his heart all a-quiver. "Tell me, darling; we are one another's."

"If I only knew that you loved me so much that—that—"

"That is just a little part of how much I love you," he replied, gently. "Tell me all!"

"You know the girl—the negroid woman—the one who painted that—horrid picture about the—'The End?'" she faltered.

"Yes, I have heard of her. Mr. Webster—"

"But you—you did not, you could not, know that—she—"

Great tears sprang to her eyes, and she turned her head away from him.

"Laura, dear girl, what can she have done to—?"

"No, no, no—not that! She, *she — is — my sister!*"

The girl shook with sobs from head to foot.

"Laura, Laura!" he cried, softly. "Listen! You must not cry so! All men make mistakes. Your father—"

"Hush! Don't mention his name! I am never to go to his home again. I—upbraided him—and—he drove me away in anger!"

He was silent in admiration of her courage.

"I left him—for—and I came to you!" she whispered, tearfully.

In a moment her head was on his breast and his trembling arms around her.

"And you shall never leave," he said, tenderly. "You are mine—mine forever!"

With a gentle thudding of pistons, the motor car stopped abruptly.

"Oakdale, Miss Lawson," the driver announced.

In the distance they could see the glow of the great electric headlight of No. 99 as it trembled and shifted upon the clouds. In a moment the brakes of the westbound limited would be grinding out their brilliant sparks against the grumbling wheels.

It was his thought—

"Why not?" he whispered, excitedly, pointing to the light in the sky.

Her eyes seemed afire with love and joy.

"Come on!" she cried, softly, clasping a full pocketbook. "We will go to the end of the King's Highway!"

"I will get the tickets!" she added, excitedly, "Luckily I have my purse."

There was a sweeping shift of the electric searchlight as the train rounded the last curve and the great engine pointed its eye straight toward the station. There was a rumble as if of Titan's steps. The sparks scintillated from the brakes. The porter sprang, with his little step in hand, to receive the possible passenger.

"Hello, Keough!" the conductor exclaimed. "You here?"

"Why not?" the reporter retorted. "Perhaps I am going farther than this with you."

"God, man! Haven't you heard the news?"

"News! What news?"

"All Atlanta is in the hands of a howling mob of murderers. They're killing negroes by the hundred! Four assaults on white women in one day! The papers are out with extras. The *Commonwealth* is leading a fight for sanity—troops called out. You are the last man on earth I would have expected to find running away from duty!"

Without a word, his face white with excitement, Roy Keough rushed to the ticket window.

"Stop, Laura—Miss Lawson! We can't go; it is absolutely impossible! Atlanta is in the hands of a mob!"

"A mob—Atlanta—" she faltered. "But I have bought the tickets."

"Then they must be returned. Here quick, agent! It is but the matter of a few days, sweetheart," he added. "You can stay at the hotel until the storm is over. Then, after duty, infinite joy!"

CHAPTER XVI

The Law of the Camp Fire

The lights of the metropolis came in sight again as the motor car rounded one of the foothills of the Blue Ridge, and soon, even above the regular thudding of the cylinders, they seemed to hear wild cries in the night. There was a volley as if from pistols fired in concert, and the dull, humming voice of the mob, soft, purring like some gigantic feline, some enormous locomotive steamed till its very ligaments vibrated—so it sounded in the distance.

The car sped on while they both trembled—one, with eager haste; the other, with black terror.

As they whizzed; the corner into Elysium Street they came full speed upon the mob. Lola Lawson fairly screamed with fright. The motor swerved unsteadily as a pistol ball whirred past the driver's head, and Roy Keough stood up in the car.

"Stop the motor instantly, Will!" he shouted. "Here, take this lap robe! Crouch down there on the floor! Keep covered! Quick!"

He threw the robe over the terrified boy and sprang into the driver's seat.

The mob was by this time all about them. The street was thronged with rioters.

Some of them saw the woman in the motor and the white man standing on the seat.

"Where's that nigger gone?" a hoodlum shouted. "Kill him, boys! He's — "

Keough understood. The mad blood lust was in these people; they were wild with the demon's craving for victims.

There was but a moment. But perhaps he had come into the kingdom for such a time as this.

"Listen, men!" he shouted. "What madness! What folly! Avenging the wrongs of our women upon the kindly, trustful, genteel negro men and women! Do you not know that none of the wild beasts are *here?* Go seek them in their lairs. And listen! If you would burn our laws and yourselves be the avengers; if by mob and murder you would forever prevent the recurrence of these awful crimes, go seek out the moral lepers of our own race who taught them how. Who are the fathers of the two million Third-Race people in this country? How many of them are *here?*"

Some of the nearest of the rioters caught the drift of his words. After all, it was they whom he wished to reach.

"While your fathers kept lonely vigil by the sad camp fires of the sixties," he continued, "who guarded their loved ones? There were five million negro friends of yours in those days, your playmates — "

He was interrupted by the pressure of the outer ring, who could not understand why the negro was not already dead.

"Aw, say now, friend," a "hillbilly" drawled, "we've got enough o' that! Hand over that nigger! He's just like 'em all; he's dangerous. Better kill him and — "

"*Dangerous!*" Keough retorted. "I'll tell you who the

dangerous men in the South are, no matter how many there be. They are white men — the lecherous, libidinous, incontinent, moral lepers who seek out the negro women to seduce them. It is as if a father betrayed his child, as if a guardian led his ward astray. These black people were ours, body and soul, for two centuries, and they have looked to us for moral law for a half century since. What ideal have we set before them? We have allowed the off-scourings of our race to set them an example of debasement, crime, lascivious rottenness. And some of these Aryan lepers have risen from their licentious beds to join decent men in condemning social equality! These I arraign. *They* are the disturbers of our peace in the South. How may we expect honor for white women when white men leave the trail of the serpent over—?"

Thus far they stood it. Then—

"Strike him down, the d——d nigger lover! Strike him down!"

"Shut up, blatherskite!" Keough retorted, while he dodged a brick. "I am a man lover anywhere, everywhere; and that is why I arraign the rottenness of the man hater, the home destroyer. I want us to teach them the LAW OF THE WHITE CIRCLE. I want—"

He dodged again as a rock came whirling by.

"To show you—you white gods—the crime of letting our rakes and whips and blacklegs lead negro women—our wards—down into the demi-monde. I—"

A brick struck his hat and carried it whirling off into the air.

He stood there then, the clean, pure Teuton, a gentleman, unafraid, his light hair fanned gently by the soft breezes from the Blue Ridge. Lola Lawson looked on him. God! For the love of such a man what would she not do?

"They come," Keough shouted again, as the mob urged themselves on upward into the car—"they come from a land where virtue was a garment to be put on or off at pleasure, where an *ad interim* wife was provided for every guest as part of his hospitality. Do you wonder, then, how rapidly they learn of our blacklegs?"

"Kill him, too!" a new voice shouted. "D——n him—the hypocrite! *He's got old Sallie Johnson's gal there with him now!*"

Keough's eyes were on fire with anger.

"Liar!" he cried. "How dare you?"

"Liar I may be sometimes," the fellow replied, grinning assuredly, "but I ain't no liar now! Take off that veil, Lola Johnson!"

A rough hand was raised to fit the deed to the word.

Keough struck out at the man, but the blow fell short. A rock hit him in the temple, and he sank, reeling, to the floor of the car.

CHAPTER XVII

The Law of the White Circle

"Lola," the voice said, "you are my promised wife, no matter if you were to be married to this Aryan. Such a marriage is illegal through all the South, as you know by your own confession in the South you would have to be married. Come, I beg—"

"Kongo, why do you not listen to me?" a woman's voice answered, quietly, but with a word of suppressed feeling. "I have told you to go away. Now I order it! What if he should wake and find me talking to one of the black folk? Go!"

"He will find it all out in God's good time, Lola," the man protested. "You cannot masquerade as Laura Lawson forever. There are scores of negroes who know you in this city who will flee everywhere from Atlanta after this riot. Your resemblance to her deceived him, and your genius planned this awful thing you have almost done. You—"

"What did you call it, Kongo? Why—"

"I called it 'awful,' but the laws would call it—'adultery!' Am I not the more considerate?"

"How dare you?" she shrieked. "Hush! Go!"

Without a word the black man turned upon his heels and vanished into the night.

Keough roused slowly from his stupor. The words kept repeating themselves in his ears. The negro man, all bruised and battered—what was it he had said? This woman, bending over him as he lay upon the pavement—those beautiful eyes—that—

"My promised wife!" Ah, those were the words! "Lola," that was the name. But this woman's was the face he loved—Laura Lawson, of Atlanta.

"He will find it all out in God's good time, Lola." The negro man had looked down at him when he uttered the words. What did it all mean, anyway? Why was he so wet and the girl all drenched there, so that her very skirts clung to her? At that he closed his eyes again.

"It was a lucky thing the fire department turned the hose on the mob," she muttered to herself, "else we had all been killed."

There was a pistol shot in the distance.

Ah, he had it—the riot!

He sat bolt upright. The woman leaned forward and touched his forehead again with a cold, wet handkerchief.

Laura—Lola? He was wide-awake now, and the negro man's words were plain.

For a moment then Roy Keough sat statue-still, while the facts—the awful, deathly facts—gripped at the throat of his soul. In the agony of it his tongue parched and his jaws gripped, as if there could never be need of words again.

"Laura," he whispered, hoarsely— "Lola, what does it mean? Why did—"

"Laura—Lola?" Had she heard aright?

In a moment the woman bent over him and was touching his forehead lightly, as if it were a pain that could be rubbed away. Even in his moment of anguish her beautiful shape and lissom grace tugged at his heart.

"My sweetheart," she began, soothingly.

"Hush, Laura—Lola!" he answered. "I know it all!"

For a moment she looked at him to read her fate. Would he reproach her bitterly? Would he do as he said he would once—take his revolver and blow his brains out?

"And yet I am the same," she murmured, softly. "I did it because I loved you so. I am the same woman you have loved."

He was silent, while the great tears sprang again to his eyes.

"It was my law, my god, who bade me do it," she continued, gently. "It was because my soul yearned for you so, and the—dream—of—you—was—so—beautiful!"

He arose and stood before her.

"That was why I did it," she said once more. "I wanted you till my heart ached."

"Lola," he began, "listen. I can't say much; for if I do, my feelings will run away with my—sense. I love you; but I am something more than myself. I am a member of the White Circle. Its law is upon me."

Keough was awake now in earnest:

The woman looked at him. This thing had come then at last, the thing whose shadow had long threatened and now cursed her as a real thing of evil. All that he had said she understood. To her there was no insult in it, only bitter pathos and unrelenting Nemesis. She, the white woman who had planned and striven to redeem herself, the black woman, told herself that he was right. That which had excluded Kongo Copelin from her life she felt and understood. To her it was only an instinctive disgust at contact with the jungle people; to this white man it was the beetling menace of the black flood. So she could understand her case, but accept it — never!

"You are sitting on a glacier, Roy Keough," she exclaimed, "gripping yourself tightly and swearing you shall not move; but all the time the icy mass is moving on — on — on. Individuals cannot stay the *end.*"

Yet, as she said it, she loved him for what he was doing, and knew that, for good or bad, he held her soul eternally. For a moment the mad joy which had been hers but a few hours before swept over her again, and her will refused to let him go.

"O, darling, Roy, sweetheart, master, don't leave me! For God's sake take me — keep me! I am — yours; do with me as you will!"

She flung herself upon his neck and sobbed it out on his shoulders.

Gently, tenderly, he unlocked her hands from about him, for the wild abandon of her love was tugging at his heart.

"Lola, you forget the great gulf — "

"Gulf!" she cried, madly. "There is no gulf too great for love!"

Again he disentwined her embraces. "It is the Law of the White Circle," he murmured. "I dare not!"

The woman stood up before him as she heard the words.

"Roy," she said, the shadow of an unexpected hope lighting her face for the moment, "take me. What does it matter about the marriage? Only love me—O, God!—you must, you shall!"

For a moment the great temptation was full upon him. Those wonderful eyes; those delicately penciled features; her form of soft, symmetrical fullness, with its invitation of infinite pleading. Ah, again those eyes which seemed able to hold all others until they were done with them! He had craved all this, and the exquisite rapture of it thralled him.

The woman took a step toward him, her hands touched his arms, her black curls were over his cheeks.

"Come," she whispered—"you love me. What matters it about the customs men have of marriage? Come!"

Then the Teuton spoke. He saw himself—Roy Keough, child of vision—the sire of a race of phallic fathers and unchaste mothers.

"Hush, girl!" he commanded. *"Do you not see that in you the crime they stoned me for telling them of is beckoning me also? Have not our white Lawsons wronged your race enough already?"* Would you have me, who am a teacher of my people—?"

Then he pitied her, for her sobs touched his heart. She, too, saw how the lecherous father and the abandoned mother had spoken in their child.

"Go back to your people," he added, gently. "Is there none among them whom you may love?"

"Immovable Folkways"

Thornwell Jacobs's *The Law of the White Circle*
and the Atlanta Race Riot of 1906

Paul Stephen Hudson

One of the most timely and unique perspectives in fiction of the growing racial tensions in the New South in the first decade of the twentieth century was a now obscure novella by Thornwell Jacobs, cryptically entitled *The Law of the White Circle*.[1] Originally published in 1907 as a popular serial in the *Taylor-Trotwood Magazine* in Nashville, Tennessee, this work—dramatically set in the time of the infamous 1906 Atlanta race riot—was quickly distributed in book form by 1908.

Author, educator and clergyman Thornwell Jacobs (1877–1956) is best known as the man who refounded Oglethorpe University in Atlanta from 1913 to 1916 and served as its president for more than thirty years. He was born in Clinton, South Carolina, and educated there at the Thornwell Orphanage and at Presbyterian College (class of 1895), both of which were founded by his father, the Reverend William Plumer Jacobs. Thornwell had known African Americans since he was a child. Across the road from the rural orphanage, on the side porch of the institution's laundry, was a dining room for many local black clientele. They were known without deliberate

insult as "Tom Scott's niggers," named after their white
employer. Thornwell always remembered with genuine
affection the older black men who were so good to him.
Driver Al Wilson, for example, could always be trusted
and depended upon to give the little white boy "many a
glorious wagon ride." Jacobs was clearly a product of the
southern white paternalism of the postbellum era. "Mr.
Scott's niggers were a precious lot of scamps but all of
us children were fond of them," Thornwell later remembered.[2]

A graduate of Princeton Theological Seminary (class
of 1899), Jacobs originally had trained for the Southern
Presbyterian ministry. After a brief, successful pastorate
at the First Presbyterian Church of Morganton, North
Carolina, and a short stint assisting his father at the
Thornwell Orphanage back in Clinton, an uncertain
Thornwell Jacobs arrived in Nashville, Tennessee, in 1906
to begin a new and misplaced career in religious press
advertising.[3]

Although Jacobs did not achieve great success in business, he encountered some remarkable literary men in
his Nashville period from 1906 to 1909. One figure was
the distinguished statesman, writer and editor Senator
Bob Taylor, who was about that time conducting a memorable gubernatorial campaign in Tennessee against his
brother Alf. *Bob Taylor's Magazine* was the first publication
to offer serial rights to Thornwell Jacobs after he wrote,
in 1906, a promising novella about the Old South and the
Civil War entitled *The Shadow of Attacoa*. Soon afterward,
Jacobs produced another serial publication, this time for
younger readers, entitled *Sinful Sadday, Son of a Cotton
Mill: A Story of a Little Orphan Boy Who Lived to Triumph,*

which was a roman à clef based on the author's boyhood years at the Thornwell Orphanage.[4] When Jacobs's mentor Bob Taylor consolidated his publication with *The Trotwood Monthly* of John Trotwood Moore, the popular southern author of *The Bishop of Cottontown: A Story of the Southern Cotton Mills* (1906), the two men formed the *Taylor-Trotwood Magazine*. In his association with this publication, Thornwell Jacobs found himself more interested in writing pieces in the magazine than in developing its advertising potential.

In two unsuccessful financial moves near the end of his stay in Nashville, Thornwell Jacobs purchased controlling interest in the Taylor-Trotwood Press and helped organize the Southern Art Publishing Company. The latter principally was to market paintings and illustrations of the noted Nashville artist Gilbert Gaul, the only southerner then part of the prestigious National Academy.[5] He was then at work on an original series depicting, perhaps systematically for the first time, romantic scenes in the life of Confederate soldiers. Jacobs subsequently was to employ Gilbert Gaul for illustrations in *The Law of the White Circle*, which gave the novella a fine artistic dimension.

By the time Thornwell Jacobs had come of age in the 1890s, strained social and racial attitudes in the South seemingly had repudiated the values expressed in the region's literature only a decade earlier. In the 1880s, southern authors such as Joel Chandler Harris and George Washington Cable had portrayed black Americans with paternalistic sympathy and tender respect, such as in the treatment of the faithful, sentimentalized figures of Uncle Remus and Marse Chan. Indeed, until the 1890s, southern whites and blacks perhaps had surprised each other and astonished their opponents by the relative harmony achieved and the good will with which they cooperated.[6] By the end of the decade, however, a genuine social crisis loomed in the South and came to the fore with the terrible race riots in Wilmington, North Carolina, in 1898. In Georgia, the brief biracial partnership led by Tom Watson and the Populists dissolved in frustration and bitterness. Legalizing the widening gulf between the races across the country was the "separate but equal" Supreme Court decision of *Plessy* vs. *Ferguson* in 1896. Meanwhile, there were in the United States imperialistic calls for ventures against peoples of color in distant lands as the northern and southern dominant white nationalistic majority truly reconciled differences by the time of the Spanish-American War.[7]

The vastly changed temper of letters in the South after 1900 reflected how established a fierce white supremacy in the region in fact had become. Thomas Dixon's trilogy— *The Leopard's Spots: A Romance of the White Man's Burden* (1902), *The Clansman: An Historical Romance of the Ku Klux Klan* (1905), and *The Traitor: A Story of the Fall of the Invisible Empire* (1907)—heralded a flourishing cult of southern Nordicism. In fields of American scholarship, particularly in sociology, the theme of deteriorated race relations was especially palpable. Using one of the most popularly accepted antiblack images, Charles Carroll published *The Negro a Beast; or, In the Image of God* (1900). Similarly, Robert W. Shulfeldt portrayed African Americans insidiously with *The Negro, A Menace to American Civilization* (1907).[8]

The southern novella *The Law of the White Circle* is singular for many reasons. Thornwell Jacobs consciously took a dispassionate, sophisticated and exceedingly complex approach even though he frankly called his work "a story of race conflict and riot." In his introductory note to the reader Jacobs deplored those observers who "had spent too large a part of their time in expostulations of negro inferiority," as had many of his contemporary writers. "The object of this book," Jacobs declared, "is not to call the negro a 'black brute,' and the Aryan a 'white angel' . . . but to give a fair interpretation of . . . our national race problem." Jacobs, however, opted to use fictional devices to make his points. After establishing his characters and a story line, Jacobs constructed the plot on a brief outline of the Atlanta race riot, although the author eschewed any documentation in the academic sense. Yet Jacobs curiously insisted that *The Law of the White Circle* was intended to be "a sociological study, not a 'problem novel.'"[9]

Although it is not clear which sociologist influenced Thornwell Jacobs the most with regard to race relations, his ideas are most akin to the distinguished William Graham Sumner, who published his classic set of lectures, *Folkways*, in 1906, the same year as the infamous Atlanta riot. Sumner contended that folkways—the ways of doing things commonly accepted in society—develop unconsciously. Vigorous folkways, Sumner believed, largely control individual as well as social undertakings while nourishing ideas of world-view and social policy. When elementary views on truth and right are developed into doctrines of the welfare of society, according to Sumner, folkways become *mores*. Although Sumner's use of his concepts was somewhat inconsistent, he postulated that folkways dominate social life. In his discussion of both folkways and mores, Sumner gave distinctions between what sociologists term "we groups" and "they groups." To attitudes of superiority concerning the folkways of "in-groups" and invidious comparison to those of "out-groups," Sumner gave the term ethnocentrism, a concept now in common use.[10]

The mounting tensions and phobias in the South, apparent with the absolute triumph of white home rule after the *Plessy* decision, were manifest in the great number of Jim Crow laws passed in the region after 1900. Georgia was in the forefront of the extension of *de jure* segregation that stretched far beyond passengers aboard trains. Only Georgia, for example, had a segregation law applying to streetcars before the end of the nineteenth century. Likewise, the state was a leader in the legal separation of the races in amusements, diversions, recreation, and sports. The Separate Park Law, adopted in Georgia in 1905, appears to have been the first venture of a state legislature in this field.[11]

"Legislation," Sumner declared, "cannot make mores, and stateways cannot change folkways." He described folkways as "uniform, universal in the group, imperative and invariable."[12] Historian C. Vann Woodward has contended that, although perhaps it was not intentional, "Sumner's teachings lent credence to the existence of a primeval rock of human nature upon which the waves of legislation beat in vain . . . when American racism was reaching its crest."[13] Applied to the southern caste system, Sumner's ideas in *Folkways* encouraged the notion that there was something inevitable and rigidly inflexible about existing patterns of segregated race relations in the first decade of the twentieth century. Indeed, in *The Law of the White Circle,* Thornwell Jacobs rendered a poignant conclusion—that since separation of the races did not originate in conscious efforts, it would be impossible for anyone to alter the fundamental existing structure of society.

Political expressions of white supremacy reached a zenith in Georgia in the gubernatorial election of August 1906. Hoke Smith, former president of the fiery *Atlanta Journal,* ran on various planks of a reform program in which he advocated the curbing of "ring" politicians, strong railroad regulation and abolition of the convict lease system. On the seemingly endless "Negro question," he forthrightly called for a constitutional amendment for the disenfranchisement of blacks, which in the white racist climate of the times routinely was considered reformist. Smith's contenders included his primary opponent Clark Howell, former editor of the relatively moderate *Atlanta Constitution.* He argued that African Americans were already in practice effectively banned from voting by the statewide "white" primary, which the Georgia Democratic party had adopted as early as 1898.[14] With his emphasis on black disenfranchisement, Hoke Smith won the Georgia gubernatorial election on August 22, 1906, with a landslide victory, in large part due to the influence of the former Populist politician Tom Watson. Although he actively had courted the black vote in the early 1890s, by 1904 Watson was a leader in the hugely popular call in Georgia for disenfranchisement of African Americans.[15] And exactly one month to the day after the pivotal election of Hoke Smith, the Atlanta race riot broke out on

September 22, 1906, which led to four days of looting, murdering and random mob violence.

Thornwell Jacobs, since his childhood days in the 1880s in South Carolina, had been fascinated with the nearby city of Atlanta, which he had frequently visited by rail. Jacobs admired "the effervescent enthusiasm of the Atlanta spirit, the rapid growth of the city, its youthful joy in breaking records of sky-scrapers," and he wanted to relocate from Nashville to what he affectionately called "the Psychic City."[16] A little more than a week after the race riot, on October 1, 1906, Jacobs stopped over in Atlanta to make a quick survey. He rode out on the Peachtree trolley to Fourteenth Street, where there was a great deal of construction of attractive homes for Atlanta's white citizens. When in passing Jacobs asked the streetcar conductor how many blacks died in the recent violence, he wearily replied, "God knows . . . my guess is about two hundred."[17] Indeed, it is difficult and perhaps impossible to know how many Atlantans lost their lives in the riot, as estimates vary wildly among contemporary accounts. The official total (which is probably far too low) was that there were twelve dead—ten black and two white—and seventy injured, sixty black and ten white.[18] "From my point of view," Thornwell Jacobs later remembered with respect to the confusion surrounding the riot, "it offered a 'natural' to the writer who dared to tell the truth about the situation which I proceeded to do as best I could." Jacobs's "sociological study" actually took the form of an impressionistic novella of which he was justly proud as "the best literary work I had done up to date."[19]

The Law of the White Circle, in the fictional sense, is a compelling story of a love triangle complicated by race, a

highly unusual premise for any white southern writer in
the early 1900s. The main white character in the book
is the handsome and intellectual but plebeian journalist
Roy Keough, who leaves the mythical town of Dunvegan
in the South Mountains (Morganton, North Carolina,
where Thornwell Jacobs began his public career).[20] Roy
goes to Atlanta and, from his first moment at the train
shed, he is deeply attracted to the city. Keough loves the
great southern metropolis with its "myriads of lights and
mountainlike buildings," which have a charming and hec-
tic appeal to the multitudes, "drawing dregs and genius
for hundreds of miles."[21] Significantly in the historic context of the Atlanta race riot, which were notoriously sen-
sationalized by newspaper accounts, Roy becomes editor
of the great morning daily *The Commonwealth*. He writes
influential editorials, becoming "the pastor of thousands
who longed for an interpretation of things."

Roy meets and falls in love with a beautiful woman
who, unbeknownst to him, is octoroon. Lola Johnson,
in the parlance of the early 1900s, is "Third Race," or
"one drop" black progeny (the term "daughter" was cus-
tomarily eschewed in the "illegitimate" context). Thus
in *The Law of the White Circle* there is an element of the
tragic mulatto theme. Black writers, notably Charles W.
Chesnutt, were exploring such topics in the early 1900s;
but Thornwell Jacobs may have been unique at this time
as a white author who dealt with such a sensitive issue.

The character of Lola, the daughter of octoroon Sallie
Johnson, was fathered by the prominent white Atlanta
dentist Dr. Lawson during his "wild-oat days." Lola is a
talented artist who had rendered a controversial, apocalyptic painting entitled "The End," on display at Atlanta's

Negro Webster University. It tenderly portrayed the peaceful triumph of the "Third Race" in an octoroon nation. Lola desperately desires to enter what Thornwell Jacobs termed the "White Circle," the social milieu of the racial majority where training, education and ambition can earn rewards and esteem. She eventually "passes" as her white half-sister Laura Lawson, who has quietly moved from Atlanta to New York. Lola is accustomed to white men's mistakenly but routinely deferring to her on the street. One day in an Atlanta skyscraper she absentmindedly enters an elevator marked "For Whites Only" instead of the car labeled "For boxes, trunks and negroes." Not surprisingly, the men aboard courteously tip their hats, and then Lola-Laura deliberately commences upon her "long dreamed madness," to live squarely within the White Circle.

Before her dramatic move, Lola Johnson had accepted the old southern folkway that "one drop [of Negro blood] may as well be a bucketful." She had pledged to marry Dr. Kongo Copelin, a distinguished professor at Webster University. The regal and confident Kongo, who descended from tribal African princes, is ebony black and has marked Negroid features. The character's first name is significant. Kongo, also spelled Congo, was the great African river and region, which for generations was known to Anglo Americans as "darkest" central Africa.[22] After the renowned white explorer H. M. Stanley had followed the course of the great river in 1876, Belgium and other western countries for decades systematically exploited the rich resources of the vast Congo domain.

Although Kongo Copelin dresses well in tailored suits and a Knox hat and is cultured and educated, ignorant whites glibly assume that he is a "big buck nigger." Indeed Kongo too knows these kinds of Negroes who educated gentlemen, black and white, consider "jungle men . . . smelly, wild, and subdued by a civilization that they fear." After Lola Johnson enters the White Circle as Laura Lawson, she rejects Kongo Copelin for Roy Keough.

Frustrated and enraged at Lola's brutal insult that he is a "Hottentot, a chimpanzee," Kongo resolves to call on her white blood father, Dr. Lawson, to let him know of his progeny's deception. The dignified Kongo, who in the heat of the moment is no accommodationist on the law of racial segregation, refuses to enter the Jim Crow back door of the dental office in downtown Atlanta. He boldly makes his way into the waiting room filled with white patients and after Dr. Lawson enters as well, tempers rise to a fever pitch. Lawson and Copelin defend themselves with their pocket knives, and Kongo unintentionally stabs the dentist in what appears to be a fatal wound.

Thinking he is a killer, Kongo instinctively runs outside past Silverman's Corner (Five Points), hotly pursued by an angry pack of white men. Kongo finds himself on notorious Decatur Street on the edge of "Darktown" in the city, where there are more than forty "dive" saloons and about 2,500 itinerant black "jungle men . . . wild beasts who could not be tamed, just like their ancestors." In this dark lair, Kongo hears the buzz of old plantation songs, filthy jokes and the curses of drunken vagrants. When a rock violently smashes the storefront window, the black men inside know it is not a routine raid but rather the hostile action of a true mob. Even though they do not know him, the "jungle men" loyally and successfully hide Kongo, whom they instantly recognize as an "eddicated nigger." The date happens to be September 22, 1906, when the awful Atlanta race riot began.

Apart from his vivid and realistic descriptions of turn-of-the-century downtown Atlanta, Thornwell Jacobs in *The Law of the White Circle* effectively reflected the paranoia of a widely reported view—that a series of Negro assaults upon white women was the presumed reason for the city's most infamous race riot.[23] For example, a graphic passage in *The Law of the White Circle* related a typically grisly story of the kind that in fact had spread throughout Atlanta. There is in the book a potent rumor that a brutish black man assaulted a fourteen-year-old white girl and her aunt, who were peacefully picking flowers near the city's Confederate breastworks. In the inflammatory account the "black beast," armed with a huge club and a large rock, viciously struck the younger girl senseless; he then, according to the story, bound the older woman, cruelly slit her face open and gouged an eyeball out of the socket. The force of these kinds of heated rumors naturally enrage the populace of white Atlantans in the novella.

Similarly significant in *The Law of the White Circle* is the role that the city's newspapers play in circulating the alleged atrocity stories. The mythical *Evening Standard* sensationally features such accounts while the rival *Commonwealth* tries to demur, believing them unsubstantiated and lacking perspective on the entire "negro problem." At an editorial meeting Roy Keough's publisher Henry Webster thoughtfully asks, "What can whites expect from another race whose women our blacklegs have deflowered so d—— shamelessly?" The relative stands of the two newspapers are somewhat exaggerated representations of the *Atlanta Constitution,* which in its morning editions generally urged relative caution compared to the more reckless evening paper the *Atlanta Journal,* as the city girded itself for the volcanic situation that had erupted between the races.

As an author ostensibly seeking a sociological perspective, Thornwell Jacobs superbly captured several salient factors involved in starting the Atlanta race riot. On September 22, the final Saturday of the summer of 1906, the downtown was flooded with white country folk. Some wanted to shop, but the vast majority were young men who planned to spend at least part of their week's wages that evening in the many saloons for whites in the city. There were also present numerous transplanted white northerners. In *The Law of the White Circle* these Yankee men in their conversations frequently speak vituperatively against the southern practice of hiring blacks as farmhands. The northern whites insist that the most insidious practice of blacks is that "they hide their criminals," a point of view that is reiterated with rising intensity as tensions mount. Some older and more responsible southern white men are in town for commerce; but the growing apprehension is reflected in guarded observations that most of them have left pistols with their wives, who are deeply concerned about the sensationally reported Negro assaults in various parts of the city, including the suburbs. Jacobs thus described the crowd ominously gathering that hot Saturday afternoon around Atlanta's Silverman's Corner as "boys, 'hillbillies' and red necks, with here and there a responsible man."

Jacobs skillfully used techniques of suspense to picture the volatility of Atlanta's downtown as nightfall descended the fateful evening of September 22, 1906. As the sky darkened, the crowd swelled from about 1,000 to 7,000 blacks and whites. The composition of the crowd, the temperance advocate Jacobs scornfully wrote, was an admixture of "white underclass and jungle men [lower class blacks] . . . other irresponsible youth, hoodlums," nearly all "drunken revelers."

In Jacobs's description of how the restive white crowd turned into a dangerous angry mob, *The Law of the White Circle* used powerful aural images to highlight the tension when street fighting broke out. Included are high-pitched cries of white newsboys relating, seriatim, the four most publicized, alleged assaults of blacks upon "Aryans" in various parts of the city, which led progressively to more surges of violence. A frequent refrain, which almost becomes a mantra, is the angry charge of northern whites against blacks, that "they hide their criminals," which the text intensifies with mighty italics. Jacobs employed the metaphor of the riot as a "storm-burst" and used as an apt image fire hoses, which the authorities in Atlanta in fact vainly tried as a corrective when the white mob went wild. Finally, "Fourth Assault!" cried emphatically by the newsboys, heralds another violent lurch in the action, as the angry white mob commences to pillage hardware stores and pawn shops for pistols and ammunition.

Jacobs related with more than a touch of sadness that in its frenzy the "white mob demon" made no distinctions whatsoever among peaceful or violent blacks. The rhythm of the language in *The Law of the White Circle* reflected highly complicated racial dynamics. Jacobs deplored the idea that whites (variously termed as "Aryans" or "Teutons") considered "negro wild beasts and negro men" as one and the same. Ironically the latter, Jacobs believed, "stood willingly as near the White Circle as they might," not like the lower sort who chose "the law of the jungle." Frustrated whites, Jacobs wrote, had decided to apply "jungle justice" to all blacks because of the repeated assertions that "they hide their criminals"; and thus the irrational objective of the white mob becomes to punish all Negroes without distinction. *The Law of the White Circle* accurately described in spirit the mob murders of innocent Negro working men, such as barbers, bootblacks and porters, even as they performed actual personal services. Indeed it is probable that as the Atlanta race riot of 1906 reached full stride, there in fact ensued an ugly "night of negro chasing."[24]

Jacobs's treatment of the white mob's pursuit of blacks down Decatur Street, inevitably in the direction of the train station, led to a climax in *The Law of the White Circle*. A terrified black man, running for his life, flees toward a distinguished white visitor who has only just arrived in town. He is Dr. Wilfong, a venerable Presbyterian minister from Dunvegan in the mountains of North Carolina, who has long been a mentor for Roy Keough, editor of the Atlanta *Commonwealth*.[25] Quickly sizing up the dangerous situation, the sympathetic Dr. Wilfong asks the black fugitive to lie at his feet in order to use the man's back as a platform and therefore to save him. (The scene perhaps uses considerable license to dramatize an unsuccessful ploy by Atlanta Mayor James G. Woodward, who mounted a box in order to speak at Pryor and Decatur streets in a vain attempt to calm the mob.) Wilfong's action startles and then calms the white mob, armed with hammers and makeshift weapons, and the minister explains that he stands on the back of the beaten and bloody Negro just as white men had done since the first Dutch ship brought black folk to the New World. Wilfong then tells a poignant idealized story of the close relations between the races in the bygone era of the romantic Old South.

The impressive old minister relates to the quieted crowd that in his younger days as a pastor there had been a former slave who had been the "boy" at the manse for the local church. One day when Reverend Wilfong had asked the gray-headed old Negro to dig up a bed of violets that appeared to be misplaced, he looked at the white employer strangely and said, "Yes, sir, boss." But after a week when the black man, even after another request, still had not done the job, Dr. Wilfong was obliged to issue a reprimand and demand an explanation. When confronted, the former slave's eyes had filled with tears as he reluctantly stated the reason for his deliberate disobedience, which author Jacobs expertly rendered in the Negro dialect of the Old South. "Boss, when me an' my marster was little boys, befo' de done buy dis ole house from him fer to be de manse, we planted dem violets dere," the faithful old black man confessed, adding simply, "I jes' done been tryin'; but I can't, boss—I can't dig dem violets up what we planted when we was boys." Indeed, the sentimentalized character represents the quintessence of his race as portrayed a little more than a decade earlier by Booker T. Washington in the Atlanta Exposition Address of 1895. The old Negro in *The Law of the White Circle* can be described aptly in Washington's own words: "faithful . . . unresentful . . . with tear-dimmed eyes . . . humble [and] . . . interlacing . . . life . . . in a way that shall make the interests of both races one."[26]

After relating his striking story, the Reverend Wilfong gives a high-minded appeal to what were known in the New South as the responsible "best elements," and he too alludes nostalgically to the presumed mutually supporting bonds between whites and blacks in the old order of the antebellum era. Wilfong affectionately addresses the fellows of his beloved region in the crowd as "Southrons" and then he asks pointedly and rhetorically: "Who will dig up the beds of friendship our fathers and theirs planted before the war?" Sheepishly the crowd disperses; and as it leaves an unchastened New Yorker, who has clearly enjoyed the excitement of the evening, callously exclaims to an Ohioan, "It was great sport chasing those niggers!"

Because *The Law of the White Circle* first appeared as a serial, it has numerous twists and "cliffhangers," and perhaps most surprising is that the wretched black man saved by the Reverend Wilfong at the train station is in fact Dr. Kongo Copelin of Webster University. Further, it is not until the grateful Negro professor learns that Wilfong's Atlanta host is the white dentist Dr. Lawson that Kongo realizes with tremendous relief that he is not a murderer and shall not have to live as a "jungle man."

The relationship between Kongo's love interest Lola, who had with daring entered the White Circle by "passing" as Laura Lawson to become involved with the white Roy Keough, is the final symbolic casualty of the Atlanta race riot. As the couple prepares to elope on board No. 99 at the railroad station, a messenger reaches Roy with information of the chaos in downtown Atlanta, insisting that the *Commonwealth* needs him. On a harrowing ride back to the newspaper office, the white mob surrounds the automobile to attack the Negro driver, and some of the rioters with indignant shouts identify the woman inside the car as Lola, the daughter of octoroon Sallie Johnson from Atlanta's Darktown.

The denouement of *The Law of the White Circle* is Roy's stunned realization that he is in love with a black woman, even though she is "one drop." He immediately knows he must end the relationship with Laura-turned-Lola. The woman knows as well that Roy is in fact correct about the gulf between the races—it is, he says, the inexorable "Law of the White Circle." In the bitter pathos the white man who once unknowingly loved the black woman faces her, both miserable and in tears, soaking wet from the fire hose that saved them from the angry mob. "Go back to your people," Roy counsels Lola, and in the wrenching, memorable final statement of the novella he tenderly asks her, "Is there none among them you may love?"

Because Thornwell Jacobs by the late 1920s emerged in Georgia as a prominent evolutionist and perhaps the state's foremost millenarian,[27] the more or less philosophical, cosmic ruminations of the characters in *The Law of the White Circle*—which as dialogue is often contrived—deserve special mention with regard to race. Many statements by characters in the book reflect standard late nineteenth-century social Darwinian ideas that influenced sociologists such as William Graham Sumner as well as the zeitgeist of the rampant white racism of the early twentieth century. Even the Negro professor Kongo Copelin, for example, believes that hundreds of millenniums unfortunately are distilled from the environment of the jungle into the pigment of Negroes. Just as the heat of equatorial Africa burned people black, he says, the cool, moist forests of northern Europe bleached the skin and hair of "Aryans." Kongo muses that as snow, cold and wind made whites survive as the fittest, so would these elements eventually enable blacks, in due course, to survive.

Kongo Copelin as an intellectual does not adopt the widespread pessimistic speculation of many thoughtful observers in the early 1900s. Atlanta University professor W. E. B. Du Bois deplored the notion that the black "race will either die out or migrate from the land . . . [in] the practical and unemotional way the Darwinian doctrine of survival is applied to the Negro problem."[28] Yet unlike Du Bois, Kongo does not demand the abolition of the color line, and indeed he has a remarkable patience worthy of Booker T. Washington. "There is no lack of centuries," Kongo optimistically consoles himself on the great question of race and survival; and although he believes it may take hundreds of years to remove "the smell of the jungle," he is in his own time encouraged by the rapid advancement of African Americans in the scant forty years since the dawn of freedom.

In Kongo's discussions with Lola, the octoroon woman ironically agrees with him. "Your race has a slow painful evolution," she maintains pointedly to the full-blooded Negro, while speculating that the "Third Race is ahead of you by a millennium." Yet Lola realizes, when she and Roy entertain the obligatory visiting northern white journalist studying the "Negro problem," that people in his region have no more desire than do southerners for a Third Race. In his section of the country, the northerner relates, there is also a "hydra-headed race problem," not only with the influx of Turkish and Chinese immigrants, but also with the rising black population of urban centers such as Philadelphia and New York. Racial amalgamation is socially dangerous and unwanted everywhere, Kongo and Lola bitterly realize at the conclusion of *The Law of the White Circle*, "as if there were a mulatto in the South whose father was not a white man."

The closed curve of what author Thornwell Jacobs so eloquently labeled the "White Circle" remained legally fixed for decades in the South, chiefly through increased numbers of Jim Crow laws in the aftermath of the great urban racial disturbances in the region at the turn of the twentieth century.[29] Less than a year after the 1906 Atlanta race riot, a triumphant Governor Hoke Smith proclaimed in his inaugural address that "any plan for the Negroes which fails to recognize the difference between the white and black races will fail." Significantly, Smith added unequivocally: "It is . . . the difference of race, deep seated, inherited for generations and generations for hundreds of years."[30] Decades later, the eminent southern historian C. Vann Woodward contended that such unchallenged doctrines that prevailed for so long in the twentieth century were "'immovable folkways' and 'irresistible mores.'" As he sought to disquiet the persistence of racial segregation, Woodward plaintively urged that "we can at least try to understand what has happened."[31] Indeed *The Law of the White Circle*, taken as a whole, ironically remains a marvelous if somewhat mysterious kind of fictional précis of what Woodward called "cross currents and contradictions, revolutionary innovations and violent reactions" in the relations between the races at the turn of the twentieth century.

Aside from *The Law of the White Circle* itself, there is little direct evidence about what Thornwell Jacobs actually

This advertisement for Jacobs's novel was distributed by the publisher just after its publication. The book achieved a measure of critical acclaim in the South, as indicated by the strong endorsement by the influential Tom Watson, who called it "a book to stir the passions . . . that powerfully grips the pillars of the social life." (Flyer from Oglethorpe University Archives)

thought of the Atlanta riot of 1906, about segregation, disenfranchisement, or race relations in general in the early twentieth century. Jacobs's self-described "sociological study" set during the Atlanta race riots was ostensibly sympathetic toward the plight of Negroes, and as a work of literature it obviously was a rather tragic piece. The overall plot of the story effectively reflected what was in all probability a pervasive view—that blacks and whites in the South in the early 1900s had become in social life deeply separate and fundamentally different from each other. The underlying operative assumptions made in the book may well have been fairly typical and indeed they were critical in the creation of a new racial order in the South.

Despite the complicated and unorthodox approach to race relations taken by Thornwell Jacobs in *The Law of the White Circle*, he subsequently became tentative and offered no more such penetrating insights on the topic. When Jacobs came to take up residence in Atlanta in the autumn of 1909, he was preoccupied with beginning a public career in white higher education in a dynamic and fascinating city that to him was "young and excited and nervous . . . breaking its own records annually and attempting new activities daily." Meanwhile Atlanta's irrepressible black citizens in the aftermath of its terrible race riot had moved east to Auburn Avenue, and they continued earlier migrations west in the city. Perhaps referring to the disenfranchisement program of his adopted state's new governor, Jacobs wrote tersely and cryptically, "Georgia had just been Hoke-Smithed."[32] The White Circle indeed was to remain as racially exclusive as Thornwell Jacobs, in his unusual but telling novella, had so well described; and in the end he, as much as any representative southern white of his generation, accepted the barrier of segregation as a seemingly immovable folkway.

Notes

1. Thornwell Jacobs, *The Law of the White Circle* (Nashville, Tenn., 1908).

2. Thornwell Jacobs, *Step Down, Dr. Jacobs: The Autobiography of an Autocrat* (Atlanta, Ga., 1945), 30.

3. See David N. Thomas, "Jacobs, Thornwell" in Kenneth Coleman and Charles Stephen Gurr, *Dictionary of Georgia Biography*, 2 vols. (Athens, Ga., 1983), 1: 126–33. On Jacobs's pastorate in North Carolina see Mark A. Huddle, *Lift High the Cross: A Bicentennial History of the First Presbyterian Church, Morganton, North Carolina, 1797–1997* (Morganton, N.C., 1997); Jacobs, *Step Down, Dr. Jacobs*, 126–33.

4. Thornwell Jacobs, *Sinful Sadday, Son of a Cotton Mill: A Story of a Little Orphan Boy Who Lived to Triumph* (Nashville, Tenn., 1908).

5. Jacobs, *Step Down, Dr. Jacobs*, 128.

6. C. Vann Woodward, *The Strange Career of Jim Crow*, 2nd revised ed. (New York, 1966), 80. Chapter 3, "Capitulation to Racism," is especially useful.

7. See Paul H. Buck, *The Road to Reunion, 1865–1900* (New York, 1937).

8. Woodward, *Strange Career of Jim Crow*, 94.

9. Jacobs, "To the Reader," October 1, 1908, *Law of the White Circle*, 9–10. Writers of Jacobs's generation did not routinely capitalize the "N" in "Negro." Corrections are not made in textual quotations in order to preserve this mindset.

10. See William Graham Sumner, *Folkways: A Study of the Sociological Importance of Usages, Manners, Customs, Mores and Morals* (New York, 1906). See also Nicholas S. Timasheff, *Sociological Theory: Its Nature and Growth* (New York, 1967), 68–71.

11. Woodward, *Strange Career of Jim Crow*, 97–99.

12. *Ibid.*, 103 (quoting Sumner, *Folkways*).

13. *Ibid.*

14. *Ibid.*, 85.

15. See C. Vann Woodward, *Tom Watson, Agrarian Rebel* (New York, 1938).

16. Jacobs, *Step Down, Dr. Jacobs*, 126–33. Jacobs terms Atlanta the "Psychic City" because he claimed it largely was "formed by invisible forces."

17. *Ibid.*, 136.

18. Darlene R. Roth and Andy Ambrose, *Metropolitan Frontiers: A Short History of Atlanta* (Atlanta, Ga., 1996), 132.

19. Jacobs, *Step Down, Dr. Jacobs*, 131. *The Law of the White Circle* garnered considerable critical and popular acclaim. The *Nashville Banner* praised Thornwell Jacobs's "new viewpoint, which is both strong and fair ... of peculiar interest in the South." Jacobs treasured a devoted fan letter from Roy V. Ellise, superintendent of the public school system of Sikeston, Missouri. Many years after the publication of *The Law of the White Circle*, Ellise wrote, he had "read it for over a quarter of a century to the upper pupils in three different high schools, thinking it the finest exposition of the Negro problem as a sociological one that I have ever read."

20. Thornwell Jacobs's first serial publication in 1906 and his first novel, *The Shadow of Attacoa*, also begins in the mythical town of Dunvegan, in the mountains of North Carolina. Jacobs later did a radical revision of the work that was published by E. P. Dutton as *Red Lanterns on St. Michael's* (New York, 1941).

21. Uncited quotations are from Jacobs, *The Law of the White Circle.*

22. H. M. Stanley, *Through the Dark Continent* (London, 1878).

23. Two of the best analytical accounts are by Charles Crowe: "Racial Violence and Social Reform—Origins of the Atlanta Race Riot of 1906," *Journal of Negro History* 53 (1968): 234–56, and "Racial Massacre in Atlanta, September 22, 1906," *Journal of Negro History* 54 (1969): 150–73. For African-American responses to the riot, see Dominic J. Capeci Jr. and Jack C. Knight, "Reckoning with Violence: W. E. B. Du Bois and the 1906 Atlanta Race Riot," *Journal of Southern History* 62 (November 1996): 727–66; and Gregory Mixon, "'Good Negro—Bad Negro': The Dynamics of Race and Class in Atlanta during the Era of the 1906 Riot," *Georgia Historical Quarterly* 81 (Fall 1997): 622–62.

24. See Franklin M. Garrett, *Atlanta and Environs,* 3 vols. (Athens, Ga., 1954), 2: 500–505.

25. The character of Dr. Wilfong in *The Law of the White Circle* is patterned after Thornwell's father, the Reverend William Plumer Jacobs. Thornwell Jacobs dedicated *The Law of the White Circle* to "my dear old father, who could have written it so much better than I have done."

26. Booker T. Washington, "Atlanta Exposition Address" (1895), in *Up From Slavery: A Biography* (New York, 1901), 218–25.

27. See Paul Stephen Hudson "'The End of the World—and After': The Cosmic History Millenarianism of Thornwell Jacobs," *Georgia Historical Quarterly* 82 (Fall 1998): 594–607.

28. See W. E. B. Du Bois, "The Future of the Negro in America," *The East and West* 2 (January 1904). Du Bois, like Jacobs in the early 1900s, used symbolic language—"the Veil"—as a metaphor for separation of the races. See *The Souls*

of Black Folk (New York, 1903). Du Bois wrote from Atlanta in the "Forethought" to his classic work: "Need I add that I who speak here am bone of the bone and flesh of the flesh of them that live within the Veil?" Du Bois's "Veil" would hang outside Jacobs's "White Circle," if the metaphors could be mixed.

29. Within two years of the Atlanta race riot, Georgia instituted its variation of the "grandfather clause" or the "good character clause" in the 1908 state constitution, and adopted the poll tax as well, all of which were enormously effective in restricting the Negro vote. See Woodward, *Strange Career of Jim Crow*, 84.

30. "Hoke Smith's Gubernatorial Address, 1907" in Paul D. Escott and David R. Goldfield, eds., *Major Problems in the History of the American South*, Vol. 2: *The New South* (Lexington, Mass., 1992), 229.

31. Woodward, *Strange Career of Jim Crow*, 109.

32. Jacobs, *Step Down, Dr. Jacobs*, 140–41.

From A Man Called White

The Autobiography of Walter White

Walter White

On a day in September 1906, when I was thirteen, we were taught that there is no isolation from life. The unseasonably oppressive heat of an Indian summer day hung like a steaming blanket over Atlanta. My sisters and I had casually commented upon the unusual quietness. It seemed to stay Mother's volubility and reduced Father, who was more taciturn, to monosyllables. But, as I remember it, no other sense of impending trouble impinged upon our consciousness.

I had read the inflammatory headlines in the *Atlanta News* and the more restrained ones in the *Atlanta Constitution* which reported alleged rapes and other crimes committed by Negroes. But these were so standard and familiar that they made—as I look back on it now—little impression. The stories were more frequent, however, and consisted of eight-column streamers instead of the usual two- or four-column ones.

Father was a mail collector. His tour of duty was from three to eleven p.m. He made his rounds in a little cart into which one climbed from a step in the rear. I used to drive the cart for him from two until seven, leaving him at the point nearest our home on Houston Street, to return home either for study or sleep. That day Father decided that I should not go with him. I appealed to Mother, who thought it might be all right, provided Father sent me home before dark because, she said, "I don't think they would dare start anything before nightfall." Father told me as we made the rounds that ominous rumors of a race riot that night were sweeping the town. But I was too young that morning to understand the background of the riot. I became much older during the next thirty-six hours, under circumstances which I now recognize as the inevitable outcome of what had preceded.

One of the most bitter political campaigns of that bloody era was reaching its climax. Hoke Smith — that amazing contradiction of courageous and intelligent opposition to the South's economic ills and at the same time advocacy of ruthless suppression of the Negro — was a candidate that year for the governorship. His opponent was Clark Howell, editor of the *Atlanta Constitution*, which boasted with justification that it "covers Dixie like the dew." Howell and his supporters held firm authority over the state Democratic machine despite the long and bitter fight Hoke Smith had made on Howell in the columns of the rival *Atlanta Journal.*

Hoke Smith had fought for legislation to ban child labor and railroad rate discriminations. He had denounced the corrupt practices of the railroads and the state railway commission, which, he charged, was as much owned and run by northern absentee landlords as were the railroads themselves. He had fought for direct primaries to nominate senators and other candidates by popular vote, for a corrupt practices act, for an elective railway commission, and for state ownership of railroads — issues which were destined to be still fought for nearly four decades later by Ellis Arnall. For these reforms he was hailed throughout the nation as a genuine progressive along with La Follette of Wisconsin and Folk of Missouri.

To overcome the power of the regular Democratic organization, Hoke Smith sought to heal the feud of long standing between himself and the powerful ex-radical Populist, Thomas E. Watson. Tom Watson was the strangest mixture of contradictions which rotten-borough politics of the South had ever produced. He was the brilliant leader of an agrarian movement in the South which, in alliance with the agrarian West, threatened for a time the industrial and financial power of the East. He had made fantastic strides in uniting Negro and white farmers with Negro and white industrial workers. He had advocated enfranchisement of Negroes and poor whites, the abolition of lynching, control of big business, and rights for the little man, which even today would label him in the minds of conservatives as a dangerous radical. He had fought with fists, guns, and spine-stirring oratory in a futile battle to stop the spread of an industrialized, corporate society.

His break with the Democratic Party during the '90's and the organization of the Populist Party made the Democrats his implacable enemies. The North, busy building vast corporations and individual fortunes, was equally fearful of Tom Watson. Thus was formed between reactionary Southern Democracy and conservative Northern Republicanism the basis of cooperation whose fullest flower is to be seen in the present-day coalition of conservatives in Congress. This combination crushed Tom Watson's bid for national leadership in the presidential elections of 1896 and smashed the Populist movement. Watson ran for president in 1904 and 1908, both times with abysmal failure. His defeats soured him to the point of vicious acrimony. He turned from his ideal of interracial decency to one of virulent hatred and denunciation of the "nigger." He thus became a naturally ally for Hoke Smith in the gubernatorial election in Georgia in 1906.

The two rabble-rousers stumped the state screaming, "Nigger, nigger, nigger!" Some white farmers still believed Watson's abandoned doctrine that the interests of Negro and white farmers and industrial workers were identical. They feared that Watson's and Smith's new scheme to disfranchise Negro voters would lead to disfranchisement of poor whites. Tom Watson was sent to trade on his past reputation to reassure them that such was not the case and that their own interests were best served by now hating "niggers."

Watson's oratory had been especially effective among the cotton mill workers and other poor whites in and near Atlanta. The *Atlanta Journal* on August 1, 1906, in heavy type, all capital letters, printed an incendiary appeal to race prejudice backing up Watson and Smith which declared:

> Political equality being thus preached to the negro in the ring papers and on the stump, what wonder that he makes no distinction between political and social equality? He grows more bumptious on the street, more impudent in his dealings with white men, and then, when he cannot achieve social equality as he wishes, with the instinct of the barbarian to destroy what he

cannot attain to, he lies in wait, as that dastardly brute
did yesterday near this city, and assaults the fair young
girlhood of the south . . .

At the same time, a daily newspaper was attempting to
wrest from the *Atlanta Journal* leadership in the afternoon
field. The new paper, the *Atlanta News*, in its scramble for
circulation and advertising took a lesson from the political race and began to play up in eight-column streamers
stories of the raping of white women by Negroes. That
every one of the stories was afterward found to be wholly
without foundation was of no importance. The *News* circulation, particularly in street sales, leaped swiftly upward
as the headlines were bawled by lusty-voiced newsboys.
Atlanta became a tinder box.

Fuel was added to the fire by a dramatization of Thomas
Dixon's novel *The Clansman* in Atlanta. (This was later
made by David Wark Griffith into *The Birth of a Nation*,
and did more than anything else to make successful the
revival of the Ku Klux Klan.) The late Ray Stannard Baker,
telling the story of the Atlanta riot in *Along the Color Line*,
characterized Dixon's fiction and its effect on Atlanta and
the South as "incendiary and cruel." No more apt or accurate description could have been chosen.

During the afternoon preceding the riot little bands of
sullen, evil-looking men talked excitedly on street corners
all over downtown Atlanta. Around seven o'clock my father and I were driving toward a mail box at the corner
of Peachtree and Houston Streets when there came from
near-by Pryor Street a roar the like of which I had never
heard before, but which sent a sensation of mingled fear
and excitement coursing through my body. I asked per-

mission of Father to go and see what the trouble was. He bluntly ordered me to stay in the cart. A little later we drove down Atlanta's main business thoroughfare, Peachtree Street. Again we heard the terrifying cries, this time near at hand and coming toward us. We saw a lame Negro bootblack from Herndon's barber shop pathetically trying to outrun a mob of whites. Less than a hundred yards from us the chase ended. We saw clubs and fists descending to the accompaniment of savage shouting and cursing. Suddenly a voice cried, "There goes another nigger!" Its work done, the mob went after new prey. The body with the withered foot lay dead in a pool of blood on the street.

Father's apprehension and mine steadily increased during the evening, although the fact that our skins were white kept us from attack. Another circumstance favored us—the mob had not yet grown violent enough to attack United States government property. But I could see Father's relief when he punched the time clock at eleven p.m. and got into the cart to go home. He wanted to go the back way down Forsyth Street, but I begged him, in my childish excitement and ignorance, to drive down Marietta to Five Points, the heart of Atlanta's business district, where the crowds were densest and the yells loudest. No sooner had we turned into Marietta Street, however, than we saw careening toward us an undertaker's barouche. Crouched in the rear of the vehicle were three Negroes clinging to the sides of the carriage as it lunged and swerved. On the driver's seat crouched a white man, the reins held taut in his left hand. A huge whip was gripped in his right. Alternately he lashed the horses and, without looking backward, swung the whip in savage swoops in the faces of members of the mob as they lunged at the carriage determined to seize the three Negroes.

There was no time for us to get out of its path, so sudden and swift was the appearance of the vehicle. The hub cap of the right rear wheel of the barouche hit the right side of our much lighter wagon. Father and I instinctively threw our weight and kept the cart from turning completely over. Our mare was a Texas mustang which, frightened by the sudden blow, lunged in the air as Father clung to the reins. Good fortune was with us. The cart settled back on its four wheels as Father said in a voice which brooked no dissent, "We are going home the back way and not down Marietta."

But again on Pryor Street we heard the cry of the mob. Close to us and in our direction ran a stout and elderly woman who cooked at a downtown white hotel. Fifty yards behind, a mob which filled the street from curb to curb was closing in. Father handed the reins to me and, though he was of slight stature, reached down and lifted the woman into the cart. I did not need to be told to lash the mare to the fastest speed she could muster.

The church bells tolled the next morning for Sunday service. But no one in Atlanta believed for a moment that the hatred and lust for blood had been appeased. Like skulls on a cannibal's hut the hats and caps of victims of the mob of the night before had been hung on the iron hooks of telegraph poles. None could tell whether each hat represented a dead Negro. But we knew that some of those who had worn the hats would never again wear any.

Late in the afternoon friends of my father's came to warn of more trouble that night. They told us that plans had been perfected for a mob to form on Peachtree Street just after nightfall to march down Houston Street to what the white people called "Darktown," three blocks or so below our house, to "clean out the niggers." There had never been a firearm in our house before that day. Father was reluctant even in those circumstances to violate the law, but he at last gave in at Mother's insistence.

We turned out the lights early, as did all our neighbors. No one removed his clothes or thought of sleep. Apprehension was tangible. We could almost touch its cold and clammy surface. Toward midnight the unnatural quiet was broken by a roar that grew steadily in volume. Even today I grow tense in remembering it.

Father told Mother to take my sisters, the youngest of them only six, to the rear of the house, which offered more protection from stones and bullets. My brother George was away, so Father and I, the only males in the house, took our places at the front windows of the parlor. The windows opened on a porch along the front side of the house, which in turn gave onto a narrow lawn that sloped down to the street and a picket fence. There was a crash as Negroes smashed the street lamp at the corner of Houston and Piedmont Avenue down the street. In a very few minutes the vanguard of the mob, some of them bearing torches, appeared. A voice which we recognized as that of the son of the grocer with whom we had traded for many years yelled, "That's where that nigger mail carrier lives! Let's burn it down! It's too nice for a nigger to live in!" In the eerie light Father turned his drawn face toward me. In a voice as quiet as though he were asking me to pass him the sugar at the breakfast table, he said,

"Son, don't shoot until the first man puts his foot on the lawn and then—don't you miss!"

In the flickering light the mob swayed, paused, and began to flow toward us. In that instant there opened up within me a great awareness; I knew then who I was. I was a Negro, a human being with an invisible pigmentation which marked me a person to be hunted, hanged, abused, discriminated against, kept in poverty and ignorance, in order that those whose skin was white would have readily at hand a proof of their superiority, a proof patent and inclusive, accessible to the moron and the idiot as well as to the wise man and the genius. No matter how low a white man fell, he could always hold fast to the smug conviction that he was superior to two-thirds of the world's population, for those two-thirds were not white.

It made no difference how intelligent or talented my millions of brothers and I were, or how virtuously we lived. A curse like that of Judas was upon us, a mark of degradation fashioned with heavenly authority. There were white men who said Negroes had no souls, and who proved it by the Bible. Some of these now were approaching us, intent upon burning our house.

Theirs was a world of contrasts in values: superior and inferior, profit and loss, cooperative and noncooperative, civilized and aboriginal, white and black. If you were on the wrong end of the comparison, if you were inferior, if you were noncooperative, if you were aboriginal, if you were black, then you were marked for excision, expulsion, or extinction. I was a Negro; I was therefore that part of history which opposed the good, the just, and the enlightened. I was a Persian, falling before the hordes of Alexander. I was a Carthaginian, extinguished by the Legions of Rome. I was a Frenchman at Waterloo, an Anglo-Saxon at Hastings, a Confederate at Vicksburg. I was the defeated, wherever and whenever there was a defeat.

Yet as a boy there in the darkness amid the tightening fright, I knew the inexplicable thing—that my skin was as white as the skin of those who were coming at me.

The mob moved toward the lawn. I tried to aim my gun, wondering what it would feel like to kill a man. Suddenly there was a volley of shots. The mob hesitated, stopped. Some friends of my father's had barricaded themselves in a two-story brick building just below our house. It was they who had fired. Some of the mobsmen, still bloodthirsty, shouted, "Let's go get the nigger." Others, afraid now for their safety, held back. Our friends, noting the hesitation, fired another volley. The mob broke and retreated up Houston Street.

In the quiet that followed I put my gun aside and tried to relax. But a tension different from anything I had ever known possessed me. I was gripped by the knowledge of my identity, and in the depths of my soul I was vaguely aware that I was glad of it. I was sick with loathing for the hatred which had flared before me that night and come so close to making me a killer; but I was glad I was not one of those who hated; I was glad I was not one of those made sick and murderous by pride. I was glad I was not one of those whose story is in the history of the world, a record of bloodshed, rapine, and pillage. I was glad my mind and spirit were part of the races that had not fully awakened, and who therefore had still before them the opportunity to write a record of virtue as a memorandum to Armageddon.

It was all just a feeling then, inarticulate and melancholy, yet reassuring in the way that death and sleep are reassuring, and I have clung to it now for nearly half a century.

A Litany of Atlanta

W. E. B. Du Bois

Done at Atlanta, in the Day of Death, 1906

O SILENT GOD, Thou whose voice afar in mist and mystery hath left our ears an-hungered in these fearful days—
  Hear us, good Lord!

Listen to us, Thy children: our faces dark with doubt are made a mockery in Thy sanctuary. With uplifted hands we front Thy heaven, O God, crying:
  We beseech Thee to hear us, good Lord!

We are not better than our fellows, Lord, we are but weak and human men. When our devils do deviltry, curse Thou the doer and the deed: curse them as we curse them, do to them all and more than ever they have done to innocence and weakness, to womanhood and home.
  Have mercy upon us, miserable sinners!

And yet whose is the deeper guilt? Who made these devils? Who nursed them in crime and fed them on injustice? Who ravished and debauched their mothers and their grandmothers? Who bought and sold their crime, and waxed fat and rich on public iniquity?
  Thou knowest, good God!

Is this Thy justice, O Father, that guile be easier than innocence, and the innocent crucified for the guilt of the untouched guilty?

Justice, O judge of men!

Wherefore do we pray? Is not the God of the fathers dead? Have not seers seen in Heaven's halls Thine hearsed and lifeless form stark amidst the black and rolling smoke of sin; where all along bow bitter forms of endless dead?

Awake, Thou that sleepest!

Thou art not dead, but flown afar, up hills of endless light, thru blazing corridors of suns, where worlds do swing of good and gentle men, of women strong and free—far from the cozenage, black hypocrisy and chaste prostitution of this shameful speck of dust!

Turn again, O Lord, leave us not to perish in our sin!

From lust of body and lust of blood
Great God, deliver us!

From lust of power and lust of gold,
Great God, deliver us!

From the leagued lying of despot and of brute,
Great God, deliver us!

A city lay in travail, God our Lord, and from her loins sprang twin Murder and Black Hate. Red was the midnight; clang, crack and cry of death and fury filled the air and trembled underneath the stars when church spires pointed silently to Thee. And all this was to sate the greed of greedy men who hide behind the veil of vengeance!

Bend us Thine ear, O Lord!

In the pale, still morning we looked upon the deed.
We stopped our ears and held our leaping hands, but
they—did they not wag their heads and leer and cry with
bloody jaws: Cease from Crime! The word was mockery, for
thus they train a hundred crimes while we do cure one.

Turn again our captivity, O Lord!

Behold this maimed and broken thing; dear God, it was an
humble black man who toiled and sweat to save a bit from the
pittance paid him. They told him: Work and Rise. He worked.
Did this man sin? Nay, but some one told how some one said
another did—one whom he had never seen nor known. Yet
for that man's crime this man lieth maimed and murdered,
his wife naked to shame, his children, to poverty and evil.

Hear us, O Heavenly Father!

Doth not this justice of hell stink in Thy nostrils, O God?
How long shall the mounting flood of innocent blood roar
in Thine ears and pound in our hearts for vengeance? Pile
the pale frenzy of blood-crazed brutes who do such deeds
high on Thine altar, Jehovah Jireh, and burn it in hell
forever and forever!

Forgive us, good Lord; we know not what we say!

Bewildered we are, and passion-tost, mad with the
madness of a mobbed and mocked and murdered people;
straining at the armposts of Thy Throne, we raise our
shackled hands and charge Thee, God, by the bones of our
stolen fathers, by the tears of our dead mothers, by the very
blood of Thy crucified Christ: What meaneth this? Tell us
the Plan; give us the Sign!

Keep not thou silence, O God!

Sit no longer blind, Lord God, deaf to our prayer and dumb to our dumb suffering. Surely Thou too art not white, O Lord, a pale, bloodless, heartless thing?

Ah! Christ of all the Pities!

Forgive the thought! Forgive these wild, blasphemous words. Thou art still the God of our black fathers, and in Thy soul's soul sit some soft darkenings of the evening, some shadowings of the velvet night.

But whisper—speak—call, great God, for Thy silence is white terror to our hearts! The way, O God, show us the way and point us the path.

Whither? North is greed and South is blood; within, the coward, and without, the liar. Whither? To death?

Amen! Welcome dark sleep!

Whither? To life? But not this life, dear God, not this. Let the cup pass from us, tempt us not beyond our strength, for there is that clamoring and clawing within, to whose voice we would not listen, yet shudder lest we must, and it is red, Ah! God! It is a red and awful shape.

Selah!

In yonder East trembles a star.

Vengeance is mine; I will repay, saith the Lord!

Thy will, O Lord, be done!

Kyrie Eleison!

Lord, we have done these pleading, wavering words.

We beseech Thee to hear us, good Lord!

We bow our heads and hearken soft to the sobbing of women and little children.

We beseech Thee to hear us, good Lord!

Our voices sink in silence and in night.

Hear us, good Lord!

In night, O God of a godless land!

Amen!

In silence, O Silent God.

Selah!

Printed in the United States
61038LVS00001B/101